By VERITY CROKER

Jilda's Ark
May Day Mine

Published by HARMONY INK PRESS
www.harmonyinkpress.com

VERITY CROKER

JILDA'S ARK

Harmony Ink

Published by

HARMONY INK PRESS

5032 Capital Circle SW, Suite 2, PMB# 279, Tallahassee, FL 32305-7886 USA
publisher@harmonyinkpress.com • harmonyinkpress.com

Jilda's Ark
© 2018 Verity Croker.

Cover Art
© 2018 Kanaxa.
Cover content is for illustrative purposes only and any person depicted on the cover is a model.

Trade Paperback ISBN: 978-1-64080-601-6
Digital ISBN: 978-1-64080-600-9
Library of Congress Control Number: 2018903422
Trade Paperback published December 2018
v. 1.0

Printed in the United States of America
(∞)
This paper meets the requirements of
ANSI/NISO Z39.48-1992 (Permanence of Paper).

To Noel—
you set off a spark in my brain, resulting in this story.

ACKNOWLEDGMENTS

THANK YOU to everyone who gave me feedback on *Jilda's Ark*, especially the wonderful editors at Harmony Ink Press—you have all helped create the final shape of this novel. To Kanaxa, I really appreciate all your efforts in designing such a gorgeous cover. To the Eastern Shore Writers and CWILLS, whose encouragement and support I will always be grateful for, I am truly indebted. A special thanks to my brother Evan Croker who is ever-generous with his insightful feedback and suggestions, and to my family and friends who never stop believing in me, I thank each of you.

Author's Note

Verity Croker writes across a variety of genres, including books, short stories, travel articles, and poetry. She has two published children's books, *Cyclone Christmas* and *Block City*, a textbook, *Grammar Worksheet Workout*, and a young adult novel, *May Day Mine*. *Jilda's Ark* is her second young adult novel.

CHAPTER ONE
DAY ELEVEN SHIP

STRONG HANDS hold me high, and I can feel myself teetering over the edge of the metal rail. The wind whips my hair around and flicks it into my eyes. Am I really going to end up in the icy-looking water far below, or are they bluffing?

I hear a cry. "Stop! Stop! Let her down!" It's the captain, who has followed us and is right behind the men. "Think about what you're doing. She is a human being who has done no harm."

"*Tell us where we are going*," yells one of my captors, "*and we will let her go!*"

A chant begins, with others on the deck joining in.

"Where are we going? Where are we going?"

Some people start to clap and stomp their feet in rhythm with the words, and soon the noise is deafening.

"*Where are we going? Where are we going?*"

The captain finally understands they really mean business. I feel myself being lifted higher, my toes now barely touching the top of the railing. The men are holding me by my calves and wrists, and it's all I can do to try and keep my balance I'm swaying so much. Suddenly I'm pushed, but my fall is broken as rough hands keep gripping my ankles. My face thumps into the side of the ship below the railing, and I can feel blood pour hot from my nose. I'm hanging upside down, outside the railing, and

1

I'm screaming and bawling at the same time, stomach rolling. My fists beat against the metallic hull of the ship.

How has our tropical island holiday turned into such horror?

CHAPTER TWO
DAY ONE SHIP

"WHY DON'T you want to come with us, Jilda?" Mum calls to me from inside the cabin. She sounds worried.

I'm leaning out over the veranda rail, gazing at the seemingly unspoiled island—one of the lesser-known islands of Fiji. Palm trees sway in the breeze, the white sand seems barely walked on, and the sun sparkles on the tropical turquoise ocean.

"I feel like I'm going to puke, and I've still got the runs. I don't think I could cope with a five-hour excursion today."

I breathe the fresh air in deeply, trying to settle my stomach.

I doubt it's the food on the cruise ship that's made me ill, and all I can think of is the street food I bought the other day in Tonga. The crab-cake burger tasted so delicious, but how long had the seafood been lying around in the tropical sun? Perhaps not such a great idea. I've been feeling off ever since, and I don't think it's just a bout of seasickness.

I've been really looking forward to exploring Fiji, but I know I won't be able to cope with the winding roads and long hours in the bus we've been warned of in the excursion details pamphlet.

"I don't like leaving you here on your own," says Mum.

"Mum, I'm nearly sixteen. I'll be fine. As if anything will happen here. I'll probably sleep most of the day anyway, and order room service for lunch if I feel at all like it. I won't even have to leave the cabin."

"She'll be okay, Mum," says my twin sister, Rosa, trying to placate her. "Heaps of people stay behind on the ship and never get off."

"Why they bother coming on a cruise if all they do is hang around the pool and never go sightseeing is beyond me," says Mum, planting a quick kiss on my cheek, before grabbing her backpack and shunting Rosa out the door. "They can do that at home."

"We'll take lots of pics so you won't feel you've missed out," cries Rosa over her shoulder, and the heavy door swings firmly shut behind them with a click.

"You can eat my share of lunch!" I call out to the closed door, though I know they probably won't hear me.

I turn to look at the view again, then after a few moments step back into the cabin and lie down on the bed. Because there are three of us, we have a suite, with a huge king-size bed in the bedroom and a sofa bed in the lounge room area. Rosa and I sleep on the large bed and Mum has the sofa bed. I lie on my back, diagonally across the bed, and sweep my arms and legs back and forth like you do to make snow angels. I'm enjoying having all this massive bed space to myself. My stomach starts to settle. While drifting off to sleep, I think about all the cool sights we've seen so far on the trip. Hopefully it'll only be yesterday and today I feel unwell, as I really don't want to miss out on any of the other islands.

I remember us choosing the cruise itinerary months ago. After much discussion we decided on one that went from Sydney to islands including Samoa, Vanuatu, Tonga, and Fiji. Mum had long wanted to go to the Caribbean, especially to St. Lucia, Barbados, the Bahamas, and Jamaica, but with the international flights added, it would all be too exy. So she gave up on that idea and was content to let us decide where we wanted to go. The holiday is, after all, to celebrate our sixteenth birthdays. After poring over different cruise itineraries for hours and noting down the pros and cons of each—Rosa did a spreadsheet, would you believe—we decided something in the Pacific Ocean would be just as special. Rosa and I wanted our boyfriends, Zac (mine) and Andy (hers) to come on the trip too, but Mum and Dad both said that wasn't going to happen. We'll all celebrate together with a party at Zac's parents' place—they've got a huge house and garden—when we get home again.

After a time I fall asleep, and when I finally awake, I have a vivid recollection of a dream in which I heard the familiar rising ding-ding-ding from the tannoy that heralds announcements, followed by the voice of the cruise director.

"Can all passengers and crew please report to the Vista Theater immediately. Repeat: all passengers and crew to the Vista Theater immediately. This is not a drill. Repeat: this is not a drill. No life jackets needed, no life jackets necessary."

I remember the lifeboat drill we had on the first afternoon we boarded the boat, with hundreds of passengers crowded into each muster station. I wondered then whether anyone would remember which muster station they were supposed to go to if there were a real emergency.

Now fully awake, I have to immediately bolt to the bathroom and am so glad I opted to stay on board. It would've been so embarrassing having to ask the bus driver to stop in the middle of nowhere and run into the bushes with everyone knowing what I was up to. Sitting on the loo, I feel like I'm swaying and after a while I realize the ship must be sailing.

That's odd. Where are the others?

I must have been asleep longer than I thought.

Leaving the bathroom, I go out onto our balcony and see we're indeed miles from shore. Fiji is just a small speck on the horizon.

Weird. The others must be up by the pool or something, leaving me in peace.

Back in the bedroom I glance at the bedside clock. It's only 1:00 p.m. Why are we already at sea?

I remember the day before yesterday when we were in Tonga. Some of the guests went on a day trip to the north of the island and the ship set sail and picked them up from there later in the afternoon. Perhaps that's what they're doing today too, and I didn't take enough notice of the plan.

I hop back into bed but can't sleep. I feel uneasy and my dream has made me unsettled, so I get up, throw on some clothes and, after grabbing my ship's key card, slip out of the cabin. The long, carpeted hallway stretches into the distance in either direction, and I glance both ways before deciding to go up to the pool.

The hallway is eerily quiet. The space outside the lifts, where normally heaps of passengers congregate, as they are either too lazy or incapacitated to take the stairs, is empty. I take the stairs, as I always like to get a bit of built-in exercise whenever I can, and reach the pool deck. There's no one dozing on the sun lounges, or aimlessly breaststroking up and down the length of the pool. Even the humongous guy who's usually in the spa bath with the whole space to himself isn't here!

There are no waiters hovering round ready to deliver drinks or hand out towels either—that's unusual.

I remember my dream, so I wander down to the Vista Theater on deck five, directly under the pool deck, to see if maybe there really had been an announcement but I'd just been too sleepy to realize. There's no one in the huge auditorium designed for a large audience.

What on earth is happening?

Suddenly I hear somebody behind me. Startled, I jump and turn around. A man I don't recognize has come into the auditorium.

His hands are shaking, and it's all he can do to keep his voice steady.

"What are you doing here? Everybody was supposed to leave."

"I didn't know...."

"Did you not hear the announcement?"

"I was asleep. I thought it was a dream. What's going on?" My voice is shaking too.

"The ship has been taken over by our group. You were not meant to still be on board. No one was, apart from a very minimal number of essential crew. Seeing as you *are* here, you need to know we will not harm you as long as you do as you are told."

I feel tears spurt into my eyes, and quickly try to blink them away. I don't want to cry in front of him. But I can't help it. I want Mum....

"Please stay calm. Do not be upset. This is a peaceful mission. We have been forced to take this action, and seeing as you are here, we will need your full cooperation."

I feel sick and my stomach clenches. Mum and Rosa would right now be enjoying themselves somewhere on the island, probably still at that outdoor lunch while being entertained by local dancers that had sounded like so much fun when we'd booked the excursion. Eating some local produce like plantains, whatever they are. Mum and Rosa would have no idea yet what lay in store for them when they return to the dock to find the ship has sailed off without them. And with me on board!

The man continues. "I am afraid that for the next few days, we will tell you only what we decide you need to know. Secrecy is paramount. But we can inform you we will not be returning to pick up the passengers and crew that were let off in Fiji."

"But my mother and sister will be worried about me!" I wail.

"They will find out soon enough that you will be fine. Where is your cabin? Does it have a view?"

I don't know whether to tell him in case he follows me there, but I know there isn't much choice. He could follow me wherever he wants—there's no place to hide on the ship where I could never be found. But I try to sound vague.

"It's a suite. With a balcony."

"Well you cannot stay there. You need to return to your suite, pack all your gear, and remain there until you are assigned a new cabin. Once you are in your new one, you will only be allowed to leave it when we call you for meals. You will be taking your dinner in the Banana Lounge—there will be no choice where you dine."

I don't care where I eat, or even know if I feel like eating, so I don't ask what's happening about lunch. I just want to be off the ship and safely with Mum and Rosa.

"Rest assured, we want you to stay safe, and you will be freed after we have completed our task."

"What task? How long will it take?"

"We cannot give any details, nor an exact time, but hopefully it will not be too long."

Finally I realize I have to do as I'm told. Despite the assurances, I know he has all the power, and I'm utterly on my own and defenseless.

"A woman will come to your cabin to show you to your new one. You really need to tell me the number of your suite so she can find you."

I mutter the number, but he seems to understand me.

I return to my cabin and begin to pack. My hands are trembling as I stuff my clothes, shoes, and toiletries into my bag. It seems so long ago that I unpacked so excitedly when we first arrived. I look around at Mum's and Rosa's things and can feel tears stinging my eyes once more.

When will I see them again?

I take one of Mum's scarves and a necklace of Rosa's that has a silver shell charm hanging from it as a bit of comfort for me. At least they'll make me feel like I have some sort of connection with them.

Soon there's a knock at the door.

"Are you ready?" someone calls.

I open the door to one of the staff members, our housekeeper Lily, who's always been so friendly to me and Mum and my sister. Whenever she sees us, she exclaims how alike Rosa and I are and tells Mum how lucky she is having us both. I feel so relieved to see her familiar face.

"How come you're still on board?" I ask. "I thought all the crew were supposed to have left the ship too."

"Yes, we were surprised when so many of us were given a special day's shore leave. They've only kept a skeleton staff. I don't know what's happening, but they've assured us we'll be fine."

"I'm scared."

"Don't be. Keep your key to this room," whispers Lily. "Hide it away carefully. You never know when you might need it. Where you are going does not have a balcony. Or even a porthole. I will give them another key and pretend it's yours."

"No porthole?"

Lily just looks at me, and I realize I must sound like a spoiled brat. I bet her cabin doesn't have a porthole, let alone a balcony.

"Thank you, Lily," I whisper, very aware of the huge favor I'm being granted and the risk Lily is taking. I slip the cabin key into my bra.

"Good place." Lily smiles, and then she leads me away.

We go to another deck and have to pass a guard standing, legs spread wide, at the entrance to the long corridor. I can see way off in the distance another guard at the other end where the corridor turns a corner. Lily opens the door to an interior cabin, which has a fake porthole looking through to an ocean scene painted on the back wall to pretend you have a view out. Ugh.

I can't believe it—there's another passenger still on board! She looks about eighty and is lying on the bed, one hand covering her eyes and the other clutching a bunch of tissues. She's sobbing quietly.

"Sorry," says Lily from the doorway. "I'm afraid you won't be able to leave this cabin unless you are given permission. The guards in the hallway are to ensure you don't leave this area."

And she closes the door behind her.

I drop my bags and turn to look at the woman on the bed. She stares back at me.

"We saved for years for this cruise," she says eventually. "And to think we were going to go on a previous one, but my husband was ill and we had to change plans."

"Where's your husband now?" I ask.

"He's at home. He's really too unwell to travel. He wanted me to still go on our trip, as it had been a dream of ours for so long. So my sister came instead to help me. And now look what's happened. I should've gone on an excursion today to see some local dancing with her, but I didn't want to bother her having to push me around in my wheelchair all day." She continues crying. "And now I don't know what's going to happen to either of us."

I sit down beside her and hold her hand. Her skin is soft and saggy.

"You're not alone. I'm with you now."

"Thank you, dearie. You seem a good girl."

"Jilda. My name's Jilda."

"I'm Sheryl."

I tell her about how my mother and sister are on the same excursion.

"I'm sure they'll all be fine. They'll be looked after on the island," I say, trying to convince myself at the same time.

"Thank you, dearie. You're so kind. But us. I wonder what will happen to us?"

"I guess we'll have to wait and see. The man said they'll only tell us what we need to know. And he promised they won't hurt us." I try to keep my voice steady.

"Let's hope they keep their promise, then," says Sheryl. "I'm much too old for all this uncertainty."

"How come you didn't leave when they called everyone to the theater?"

"I wasn't sure what was going on, and thought I'd wait for further announcements. But none came. It's too far for me to get to the theater without someone pushing me, and I knew it would take forever for me to hobble there."

That makes sense. I wonder if there are any other passengers left, apart from us, who for one reason or another didn't make it to the theater.

I let go of her hand and stand up and walk around the cabin, discomforted by not having any real windows in the room. I've gotten used to having a balcony, fresh air and a view, and now that I'm stuck way inside the ship with nothing to look out at, I feel a bit claustrophobic. I know our being in an interior cabin is a wise move on our captors' part, as we captive passengers have no idea where we are. The only time we'll see outside is when we're allowed to go for meals.

I'm grateful I'm not on my own, though, as my thoughts would have driven me crazy. At least I have someone to talk to, even if she is old enough to be my grandmother. But she is granny-like in the nicest of ways.

Eventually a call comes over the loudspeaker for us to go to dinner.

"I'm not hungry," I say.

I still feel a bit weak from my food poisoning, if that's what it was, and also worried about what's happening with the ship. The man said not to worry, but the uncertainty is driving me nuts. And I know Mum and Rosa will be feeling sick not knowing what's going on. Hunger is the furthest thing from my mind.

Sheryl hoists herself up in the bed and says, "I'm starving. I tried to order room service at lunchtime, but nobody answered the phone. We must always eat when we're offered food. We don't know what's happening and whether the feeding will suddenly stop, so we must keep up our strength and eat whenever we're given the opportunity."

I suppose she has a point. Who knows what's going on and whether the food will run out if we don't call in to another port to get fresh supplies. Although there aren't that many of us on board by the look of things, there still seems to be some staff who'll also need to eat. Not all of them were told to take the day off in Fiji.

Sheryl puts her legs over the edge of the bed, stuffs her swollen feet into rubber flip-flops, and, after levering herself up with a grunt, hobbles over to her wheelchair.

"I don't need it all the time," she explains, "but I do need it when I have to walk long distances."

I don't think going to the Banana Lounge is a long distance at all, especially if you use the lift, but I'm not going to try and convince Sheryl to walk in case something happens on the way.

How will I lift her up off the floor if she falls?

"I'll push you."

"Thanks, dearie. I'm so lucky to have you with me."

I'm starting to wonder whether that's *why* they put me in with her, as she seems to need a lot of help.

Pushing the wheelchair isn't so difficult, and I realize how easy it is to be on a boat with a wheelchair, as every surface is flat and there are lifts between floors. Maybe that's why so many oldies go on cruises.

There are a few other passengers still on board who mustn't have heard the announcement either, or not followed it for one reason or another. We sit near each other at two tables. It's such a different atmosphere from the previous nights when the room had been full of passengers chattering loudly and having fun. I look around at the others. Most of them appear anxious, and don't seem to have much of an appetite either. There's a friendly-looking girl with long, curly brown hair at the other table. She looks about the same age I am, or maybe just a little older. I wonder who she is, and hope I get a chance to talk to her some time. I could do with a friend my age. I'm already missing Rosa so much, and it's really only been a few hours.

I pick at the food as well as I can and manage to force down some pasta and a couple of meatballs smothered in rich tomato sauce, which fill me up.

"Veggies too, dear," says Sheryl. "Health is now your top priority."

I fork up a few pieces of fresh tomato and a couple of slices of cucumber. Sheryl smiles to herself.

Dinner over, there are no more announcements, despite several passengers demanding some answers. Some are particularly annoyed the Wi-Fi hasn't been available since the ship left the port. Even the televisions are not working, so we can't watch any news to find out if anyone knows about us. There seems to be some sort of communications blackout—at least for us.

There's no entertainment tonight, the bars are closed, and we have to return directly to the cabins. Usually we enjoy a choice of activities, like singing, dancing, music, a film, or a show. It's eerily quiet as I wheel Sheryl back to our room.

Sheryl lies down on her bed, and I sit in one of the lounge chairs. I'm putting off lying down for as long as possible, as I don't really want to sleep so close to a virtual stranger, but ultimately I know I won't have a choice. Luckily our beds are separated with at least a little bit of space in between them, though not much.

I'd brought the third book in my current favorite trilogy with me on the cruise, but I just don't feel like opening the pages. Instead I sit there with my book in my lap and think about Mum and Rosa.

What are they doing now? What do they think has happened to me?

I know Mum will be really freaking out by now with worry, and Rosa won't be much better. I wish I could let them know I'm all right—so far, anyway.

After a while I put my book on the little coffee table, get up out of the chair, and try to push my bed a bit farther away from Sheryl's. I have to move my bedside table first, which is easy, but the bed takes quite a lot of effort. I finally manage to gain an extra half a meter or so. She has her eyes shut, so I hope she won't notice what I'm doing and be insulted I want more space between us.

Sheryl begins to snore lightly, and then gets louder and louder. *Oh, no. I'm going to have to listen to her snore all night!* Eventually she wakes herself up with a snort.

"Damn," she says, and reaches for her CPAP machine—one of those appliances that help with sleep apnea. My grandfather's got one of them, so I know roughly how they work. Placing the mask over her face, she switches on the machine, and soon rhythmic breathing fills the cabin. At least it's better than the sound of snoring. She doesn't seem to have noticed the beds are farther apart.

I grab my book and hop into bed, but I lie there staring at the ceiling. Eventually I give up and drop the book on my bedside table, turn out my bed lamp, and close my eyes. The rocking boat begins to lull my senses; my eyes grow heavy and I drift off to sleep too.

CHAPTER THREE
DAY TWO SHIP

I WAKE with a start to a rat-a-tat-tat on our door. I struggle out of bed and open the door. There is breakfast on a tray for the two of us, carried by one of the ship's staff members.

"I thought we were going to the Banana Lounge for meals," I say.

"Only dinner, when it's dark" is the reply.

So they're keeping us inside during all the daylight hours—so we can never see where we are.

The scrambled eggs on two pieces of toast (one wholemeal piece and one white) are perfect—maybe because the cooks are only catering for such a small number of people. There's a mini packet of cereal each, some milk in a silver jug, a banana and strawberries, two little pots of yogurt, two large muffins (one plain and one with chocolate chips) and pots of tea and coffee.

"So thoughtful," says Sheryl, tears glinting in her eyes. "The cooks have given us a kind of choice, even though we didn't get to select what we would have."

I explain to Sheryl how I can't face coffee in the morning and have to have the tea. Luckily Sheryl is a morning coffee person.

"I can't stand the smell of tea in the morning," says Sheryl. "So that works out well for us, then."

16

"You're just like my sister, Rosa. She's like that."

My eyes blur with tears thinking of Rosa in her pajamas, drinking coffee out of her favorite mug, but I try to push that image from my mind.

I'm a little hungrier this morning, so that's a good sign in more ways than one. My illness must be over, and maybe I'm starting to cope better with the stress of not knowing what's happening. Sheryl is right—we have to keep up our strength for whatever lies ahead.

Our tray is soon bare, only a few scattered crumbs and a little drop of spilled milk left.

"Good girl," says Sheryl, patting my knee.

When I go to put the tray outside our door, I look up and down the corridor. The guards are still in place. We are truly prisoners in this cabin.

I flop back on the bed with a sigh.

"Where's your book, dearie?"

I decide that as sweet as Sheryl is, I can't stand her calling me "dearie" all the time.

"Please, I'd really rather you call me Jilda."

"Okay, dear… Jilda. How do you spell that anyway. *J-I-L-L-D-A*?"

"Yeah, that's almost right. Only one *L,* though. Mum apparently wanted to spell it the proper way, *G-I-L-D-A*. It's Italian, but Dad said everyone would say the *G* like in 'girl' and mispronounce it. So Dad got his way—probably the only time he ever did!"

I laugh in spite of myself. Mum and Dad broke up years ago, because they could never agree on just about anything. Although they *had* agreed to go halves for us girls on this trip so we can celebrate our sixteenth birthdays in style. I try not to think about the fact it's only a couple of days till our birthday.

"Where is your father? Is he in Fiji too with your mother and sister? You didn't mention him last night."

"Oh, no. He's in Hobart."

"Why is he there?"

"That's where we come from. Tasmania."

"Oh. I thought you must have been from Italy. With your Italian names, you and your sister."

"Mum and Dad had their honeymoon in Italy. That's why they wanted Italian names for us. That was in their romantic young days."

"They're not romantic anymore?" asks Sheryl, sounding wistful.

"No, long divorced."

"Oh, I'm so sorry to hear that."

"It's better really, without them fighting all the time."

"So, you live in Hobart? That is a long way indeed. Fancy that. We only had to catch a taxi to the port in Sydney to get on this ship."

"You're lucky. We had to fly from Hobart to Sydney first, and then hang out overnight at a hotel. The next morning we were so excited when we finally got on the boat. We raced along the corridor, searching for our cabin. Mum was convinced they would've made a mistake with the booking and not given us a cabin with a balcony. When we opened the door to our suite and Mum saw the balcony, she ran to the rail and grabbed it and started to cry with relief."

I feel like I'm running off at the mouth, but it seems so long since I've had a proper conversation with anyone.

"Your mother sounds like a wonderful person. So in tune with her emotions."

"She has to be. She's a writer. A poet, actually."

"My sister is too! How amazing."

"My sister is amazing too," I say. I start to cry. Sheryl pats my hand.

"Tell me about your sister, Jilda."

So I tell her all about Rosa, and the fun and close connection we have as twins. She lets me talk and talk until finally I stop.

She smiles.

"My sister is my twin too," she says.

"No way," I say. She's let me talk for such a long time, and never once interrupted to tell me she's also a twin. What a nice person she seems to be.

She begins to tell me all about their experiences as identical twins. How they had tricked their teachers, their friends, and their boyfriends. I can't believe an old person like her had as much fun as us doing such similar things when she was young so long ago.

I feel a bit closer to Sheryl now, but there's no way I'm going to tell her about our boyfriends yet. She'll probably think we're too young anyway.

After that I feel a bit more relaxed, so I pull out my book and start to read. This fills in the time until lunch, when once again a tray is brought to our room. It looks like the only excitement during our day will be what we're given to eat. This time it's sandwiches, again a choice of types of bread and fillings, some cakes, and a variety of fruits to choose from. Drinks are a choice of apple or orange juice. Well, at least our captors aren't making us starve. Or die of thirst.

But what on earth are they up to? We can tell the ship is constantly on the move. Sometimes it seems we're in fairly calm waters, and at other times, the ship seems to develop more of a roll as if out on the wide, wild ocean. Deep in the interior of the boat, in a cabin with no windows, we can hear and see nothing of the outside world. Zilch. Zip. Zero. We don't know if we're near other islands in Fiji, or way out to sea.

What are the authorities doing about us? And when will we find out what's going to happen to us? They can't keep us on this ship forever, and they said they'll eventually free us. Something will have to change. But when? And how? And why is this happening to us?

The afternoon drags on much longer than the morning did. Sheryl and I occasionally speak, and eventually she drifts off for a short nap. I do the same for a while, although how I manage that I don't know—my head is swirling with all the possibilities of what could be going on. I read another chapter of my book, but I can't concentrate on it, and all the characters and their motives get mixed up in my head.

Finally the pounding on the door signals our release from the cabin. I'm starting to understand the term "cabin fever." Dinnertime. A break in the monotony. I'm almost thankful to our captors for letting us out. I've heard about that phenomenon. *Stockholm syndrome*? Something like that. I wish I could google it, but without Wi-Fi research is impossible. But I'm determined not to feel one ounce of gratitude to those who are denying us our freedom and our families.

What I eat tonight is just whatever I stuff in my face. I've lost all interest in food, apart from the fact it's keeping me going. I put savory and sweet things together on the same plate and eat at random.

But Sheryl, I notice, is very careful to eat a mixture of vegetables, salad, and meat. And she has fruit for dessert. She's obviously trying to maintain a healthy diet. She looks at my plate, but fortunately says nothing. I think I'm in the mood to throw it at her if she comments on my choices, and perhaps my face tells her that. Because she doesn't bug me about what I eat, I decide to eat a big red juicy apple. We catch each other's eyes over the top of my apple and smile. I also catch the eye of the girl sitting at the other table. She picks up a red apple too, rubs it on her T-shirt sleeve to give it a bit of a clean, and then bites into it. We smile at each other. My stomach flops over.

Why am I feeling like this?

After dinner one of the passengers tells a guard we all really need some exercise. Hanging round our cabins all day and just coming out for dinner is quickly going to turn into a health issue.

"Constipation for a start," says Sheryl.

Good on her. She isn't shy about stating the obvious. Maybe you get braver when you get older, and don't care so much what others think.

The guard nods and goes off to talk to his superior. We all wait expectantly to hear the outcome. When the guard returns, he says we're allowed to walk around the promenade deck twice and then we'll have to return to our cabins.

It's so beautiful out on the deck in the cool night air. Millions of stars seem to almost pop out of the sky, and the wake at the back of the boat streams out behind us in an ever-narrowing white cone shape into the distance. If it were a normal night, we passengers would have been enthralled by the sight. But it's far from an ordinary night. By the light of the moon, which casts a glow over the water, we can see we are completely surrounded by ocean, not an island in sight.

Where are we and where are we going? And why?

Sheryl tries to walk a bit to get some exercise, but she's so slow she gives up and gets back in her wheelchair. People take turns helping me to push Sheryl along, which is so kind, as I really need a good leg stretch after being cooped up in our cabin for two days. I notice the red apple girl isn't in the walking group, though. I wonder what's happened to her. You'd think she'd love getting out on deck in the fresh air. Then again, what do I know about her? Nothing. Nothing apart from the fact she's stuck on the boat the same as I am. And that she likes red apples.

And she makes me feel strange....

We're finally taken back to our cabins, and seeing the guards still stationed there reminds us of our total lack of freedom.

Sheryl and I don't have much to say to each other that evening. Our walk on the promenade has reminded us of just how much our lives have changed, and in such a short time. I have a shower, and while I'm in there I have a little weep. I remember Mum saying after her first shower on the ship that the shower cubicles are so small, you only need to put soap on the walls and spin yourself around to get clean. I do a careful little spin in the shower, thinking of Mum, and after turning, lean my head against the wall of the shower and give in to my feelings. I've been trying so hard to seem positive in front of Sheryl and the others, but all this worrying and not knowing what's going on is really getting to me.

I finally stop sobbing and turn off the water. After drying myself, I pull on my soft old T-shirt and cotton shorts I love to sleep in and look in the mirror. No trace remains of my crying, and I'm glad about that, as I don't want Sheryl to notice. I come out of the bathroom and hop into bed. Reading my book helps me to become drowsy, and finally I slip away into oblivion. I wake in the night after a nightmare about Mum and Rosa struggling in the wake behind the boat, calling out to me, hands waving in the air, heads bobbing up and down in the water, almost drowning. That's it for sleep for me for the remainder of the night. The purr of Sheryl's sleep machine keeps me company as I stare into the dark.

Chapter Four
Day Three Ship

IN THE middle of the night I wake up. Something is different. After lying there for a while, I realize what it is. The ship has stopped moving! We've been constantly on the move since we set off from Fiji, but now there's no motion, and no sounds of the ship's deep inner creaks and groans. All is silent and still, and my ears are roaring with the quiet. Not being able to look out is so frustrating. I wonder whether we've just stopped in the middle of the ocean, or whether we've actually called into a port.

Sheryl rolls and mumbles in her sleep, then starts to wake up. She pulls her mask off her face, and with an annoyed grunt, throws it aside and levers herself upright in bed. I guess she's getting up to go to the toilet.

I say, "Do you think that we've stopped?"

Sheryl sits and ponders for a moment.

"I think you're right. It's very eerie."

"I wonder if they're going to let us get off. If we're in a port, that is."

"That would be a dream come true. But I'm sure they would have told us to pack before we went to bed if that were the case. I wouldn't get my hopes up."

Sheryl staggers off to the toilet. When she comes out she says, "It's funny walking without the ship's movement under your feet. You almost feel like you're still moving."

"I've heard that when people get off after a long time at sea, they walk in a funny way, as if they're still trying to get their balance."

We chat for a while, and every now and again we wonder whether we hear a distant metallic clang or whether it's just our imagination. It's so frustrating being in our enclosed cell. After a long while we drift off to sleep once more. When we wake, the ship is moving again, the now familiar rise and fall of the bed underneath me almost comforting. We speculate whether the stillness was merely an illusion. But I'm positive we had stopped somewhere.

I wonder why.

It's so strange spending my last day as a fifteen-year-old with a woman I didn't know existed a week ago. But Sheryl is a comfort to me. She tells me stories of her long-ago youth to help pass the time. She remembers her and her twin sister's sixteenth birthday and says they were given a pair of stockings each, with a seam up the back, which was the latest thing at that time. She tells me about how they used to have to hold stockings up with underwear things called suspender belts that had clips on them to secure the nylon—it all sounds so archaic and uncomfortable. I'm so glad we have tights—not that I often have to wear them. And I don't really like the scratchy feel of them anyway.

Our only real relief during the long day is breakfast and lunch. As usual. It's just so monotonous as the day drags on with no action, and not knowing what's happening.

Finally the day draws to a close. Over dinner, there is some muttered, agitated talk among some of the men about trying to overcome our captors, but we don't know whether they have guns or knives secreted somewhere, although we haven't seen any. We know, though, that whatever we do, we'll be outnumbered and could be overpowered, so it would be just dangerous and pointless, achieving nothing. We may even be put in a worse situation if we try anything. They've said they won't harm us if we stay calm, and so far that's proving to be true. It's decided it's best to be compliant for the time being, at least until we have more of an idea what on earth is going on. We don't want to tip the balance over into the possibly perilous unknown.

I notice the apple girl looking at me from the other table, and I smile and look away again quickly. It feels strange holding her eyes for too long. They're an amazing green, like sparkling dark emeralds. I've never felt strange looking at girls before....

I wonder whether she'll go on the promenade walk tonight. I hope so.

Dinner over, I push Sheryl out to the deck for our evening walk. The group is the same as last night and the apple girl still doesn't come with us. I wonder what's going on with her. Doesn't she like exercise? She looks quite fit, though. Something weird must be going on. You'd think she'd be busting to get out in the fresh air after being stuck inside all day and all night.

I look up at the moon and take comfort knowing that the same moon is floating above Mum and Rosa wherever they are, and Dad in Hobart too. The walk is over and we return to the cabin with nothing to look forward to except another long night of not knowing where we are or what's going to happen to us. And today had been the last day Rosa and I would ever be fifteen, and I'd had to spend it without her....

Chapter Five
Day Four Ship

I WAKE up this morning to a very strange sensation. It's my sixteenth birthday, so I'm supposed to be super-excited. Uber-excited even! This is the day we'd been planning toward when we booked our cruise. We were supposed to be spending today at the beach on another Fijian island. Mum told us she'd bought new bikinis for us to wear today. She'd said that it would be the one day when she wouldn't harp about wearing our rashies to protect us from the sun, but she hoped we'd be sensible and smother ourselves in sunscreen (and reapply regularly, as she kept repeating, like she was stuck on a loop).

I lie in bed for a while, thinking. This is the first birthday I've ever spent without Rosa, and it almost physically hurts she isn't here. I've never had a birthday without Mum either, and even Dad, as he always makes sure he sees us on our one special day of the year. Mum reckons Dad is always overgenerous with his gifts, implying that he's trying to make up for not being around. But we know that it was Mum who asked Dad to leave, not the other way around, so he has nothing really to make up for. That's the way I see it, anyway.

This year they're both being extremely generous, giving us this trip. Dad told us he'd given Mum a "little extra something" to give us to open on the actual day. Now I am really intrigued.

What had he got us? I know we would each get the same thing; he's always like that—treating us equally.

I decide I'll have to try and have as good a day as possible under the circumstances. It's not every day that you turn sixteen, after all. I hop out of bed and select one of my favorite dresses to wear. It's dark pink and floaty. I have my shower, wash and dry my hair, tug on underwear, and slip the dress on over my head. I'm still a bit shy in front of Sheryl and like to get dressed in the bathroom. She doesn't care, though, and always changes in the main part of the cabin.

"You look nice," says Sheryl when she sees me emerge from the tiny bathroom.

I twirl around to show off my dress. It feels soft and silky. A special dress to mark my special day. I'm planning to wear it to the party we have with our boyfriends and other friends when we get home too—but now of course I'm worried more about *if* than *when*. I grab up Rosa's shell charm necklace I took from our cabin, put it around my neck, and tie up my hair with Mum's scarf. At least I feel a bit of a connection to both of them now, even though I'm not with them. I wonder what Mum and Rosa could be doing today. Will they celebrate our birthday without me? It's inconceivable to imagine.

While Sheryl is taking her shower, I remember our key that Lily let me keep. I've hidden it in my bedside table, in some tourist literature I found by the television. I get it out and finger it then, on a whim, tuck it into my bra. I've never told Sheryl about the key, as I don't want her to be aware of something she's probably better off not knowing about. I'm wondering whether there's the slightest chance of sneaking into our suite, as I really want to see my birthday presents. They're probably in Mum's suitcase, hidden in one of the pockets.

Sheryl knows it's my birthday, and after we've had our breakfast, she tries to make the time pass for me. She'd been to a towel-folding demonstration earlier in the cruise and bought a book that shows you how to do it. Before the ship had been taken over, Lily always folded one of our bath or beach towels into an animal shape and put it in the center of the main bed for us to admire when we returned after a day out or after dinner. One day there was even a large monkey-shaped one she'd made out of two towels hanging from the rail in front of the shelf that protected the glasses from sliding off in heavy seas. She'd stuck large paper eyes on the shapes, which gave them character. I'd thought it was a bit silly, but quirky in a way too. I miss those little touches of Lily's.

Sheryl convinces me it's a good way to pass the time, so seeing as I'm pretty bored, I start to copy her movements. Sitting cross-legged on the bed, I try making an elephant, a monkey, a tortoise, and a dog. We make the eyes out of torn-up ship stationery, and I color in the pupils with a pen. They actually look quite cute, and we're pleased with our handiwork. I look forward to the day I can show Mum and Rosa my new skill. But I'm starting to wonder when that will finally be.

Sheryl can see I'm feeling a bit wistful.

"You need some photos of you on your special birthday," she says. "Have you got a camera?"

So she takes a few photos of me. Then she says something which really surprises me. "Let's take a selfie."

I didn't know old people even knew what a selfie was. We huddle together holding up a couple of the towel animals. When I look at the photos later, I can't believe how happy we look. You'd never know what uncertain circumstances we were really under at the time.

Lunch helps break up the monotony of the day. After lunch Sheryl and I lie on our beds to rest. After a while I take off my dress and hop into my pajamas. I hope the apple girl will think I look nice in my dress, and I don't want it to get too crushed before wearing it to dinner tonight.

Sheryl drifts off. I'm not in the least bit tired, and I can feel the cabin key in my bra. I wonder if I'll ever have a chance to use it. And today of all days—I really want my presents. The afternoon drags by. What a fizzer of a birthday.

Finally we're called to dinner. Sheryl tells the others it's my birthday, so they get a large slice of cake and put it in front of me. There are no candles, but one of the passengers lights a match and gets me to blow it out. Then I cut the piece of cake as they sing "Happy Birthday." I notice the brown-haired girl staring at me. My stomach does that strange flip-flop again. I smile tentatively at her, and she grins broadly back. I notice a little gap between her front teeth.

Why am I noticing that?

But more than anything else, I really just feel like crying. I've never had "Happy Birthday" sung just for me. It's always to both Rosa and me together. Everyone sings our names in a different order so the names always sound jumbled up, but that's how we like it. Neither of us comes first.

Tonight my chance to slink into our old cabin presents itself. On our postdinner promenade deck walk—again the girl doesn't join us—Sheryl is being pushed by one of the other passengers, Gavin, and I'm walking beside them, enjoying the break from pushing. As we're passing a doorway to the interior, I notice the guard behind us stop to turn away and put his back to the wind so he can light a cigarette. I put my finger to my lips and mouth a *shhh* to Sheryl and Gavin. Their mouths drop open, but fortunately they say nothing. My face must be telling them to shut their traps. I pull at the door. It's a heavy wooden door and the wind is buffeting against it, but I'm determined. I use two hands to yank it open, and slip through quickly, hoping the bang as it closes will be muffled by the sound of the roaring wind. I know I don't have long, but I have my excuse ready. I'll claim I feel seasick and am looking for a bathroom. It would be a fair enough excuse, as the seas are up and it's pretty rough. Some of the other passengers complained they felt a bit queasy at dinner, so they were even more keen than usual to have a walk outside on the deck to get some fresh air.

I remember exactly where our old cabin is and run quickly down two flights of blue carpeted stairs to our suite level. I'm not going to hang around waiting for a lift and be sprung somewhere I'm not supposed to be. It seems only yesterday that Mum, Rosa, and I walked along this corridor, searching for our room and seeing Mum's relief that we did indeed have a balcony. I find our cabin and, hands shaking, slip the key card into the slot. The green light pings on, I push open the door, and I'm in. I insert the key in the electricity slot and the main cabin lights come on.

Somebody's been in our suite! Everything's been tidied up, our bed is made, and Mum's sofa bed is made up as if for two people. But there are also two more mattresses on the floor covered with bedding too.

Who's sleeping in our suite?

It looks like six people are staying here now. But it's so immaculate it looks as if no one's been using the room at all. There are no personal items or luggage.

What's going on?

Not one of Mum's or Rosa's things is to be seen either. I go into the bathroom and it's the same deal there. All spotless as if ready for another group of passengers. A huge pile of clean, fluffy white towels lies on one end of the basin and more hang over the rails. There are enough towels for about twenty people. Many more than we had before. Weird. Back in the main part of the suite, I yank open the wardrobe doors and discover Mum's and Rosa's suitcases and hand luggage are neatly stacked inside. At least they haven't been taken away or thrown overboard.

I quickly drag out Mum's suitcase and unzip it in one long movement. There's a mixed bundle of Rosa's and her toiletries that have been thrown in willy-nilly. So that's where they've gone.

I pick up some of Mum's clothes and crush them into my face, trying to feel close to her. I can smell Mum. She always smells like that rose-scented bodywash she loves to use. I feel so near to her, yet so far apart, and have to hold back a sob. But I have no time to sit and think about Mum. I feel bad rifling through her things, but this is what I've come for, after all. In a pocket in the lid of her suitcase, behind her underwear, are four small gift-wrapped presents. There are no tags on them to say which are for me, and which for Rosa. I know immediately from past history they'll be the same, so take two differently shaped packages. I push them into my knickers, one over each hip bone. Luckily my dress is swirly and not close-fitting. I zip Mum's bag closed, push it back in and jam the wardrobe door shut.

I suddenly remember the safe. I didn't think about the safe when I was told to pack up all my stuff the other day, but now I think it might be a good idea to take our passports with me to keep them together. I remember the sequence— Mum insisted we memorize it—and the safe door swings open easily. I stuff the three passports into my knickers, and then I see Mum's mobile phone. Phone! I can ring Dad! I try to ring Dad's number, but then I realize I don't know the international dialing code for Australia. Maybe Sheryl can help me out.

So I slip the phone under my knicker elastic as well. I'm starting to feel quite fat. I close the safe, securing it with our special code, as there are a few more things like plane tickets and hotel booking details in there I think should stay secure, then whip the room key from its slot. The room immediately becomes dark, and I pull the door open and gaze up and down the corridor. No one in sight, so I tear up the corridor, up the two flights of steps, and peer through the window of the promenade deck door. All clear.

Fortunately the group has just walked past on their second rotation of the deck, and the guard has gone to the front. I resume my place at the back beside Sheryl. She gazes up at me but knows better than to say anything. I know she'll wait until the privacy of our cabin to find out what I've been up to. Gavin, who's still pushing her and hasn't handed her over to someone else, has enough brains to keep his mouth shut too. I've done it!

Back in our cabin, I go straight into the bathroom and lift up my dress to pull out the gifts, phone, and passports held firmly by my knicker elastic. I put the passports on the vanity unit, then sit down on the closed toilet lid and put my gifts in my lap. I open the soft package first, as I know that will be the bikini from Mum. If we were all together, she would have held the two identical packages behind her back and got us to choose which hand, so chances are I could have ended up with this one as much as the other that would be Rosa's anyway.

It's so pretty. I hold the bra top up by the straps, then pick up the bottoms and turn them back to front and back again to get a good look at them. I even turn them inside out. They're reversible. Ever the practical mother, giving us each two bikinis in one. Covered in brightly colored tropical flowers and birds on the outside and plain green on the inside, the bikini would have looked absolutely fabulous on the beach in Fiji. I wonder what Rosa's is like. I know it wouldn't look exactly the same. Mum has never bought us identical clothes, even when we were young. She said she wanted us to develop different personalities and not be clones of each other. We've sort of mucked that up over the years by sharing, but her intention was still there when she bought us clothing.

I put the bikini in my lap and pick up Dad's gift. It's hard and small. Tearing off the paper reveals a little blue box. I open it up and gaze at what's inside. A pair of mismatched earrings.

Dad... you want Rosa and me to decide which pair we prefer....

One earring is a silver seahorse with insets of what look like tiny pieces of opal, and the other is a silver turtle, also with opal insets. I start to weep, resting my head in my hands. This would have been such a fun day if Rosa and I had been together with Mum. We would have paraded our new bikinis around our suite before hitting the beach and laughed while dangling the earrings from our ears with a mock argument over which earrings we wanted.

I love them both and slot them straight into my ears. Grabbing a fistful of toilet paper, I wipe the tears from my face and stand up. I toss the paper into the bin and look in the mirror. My face is puffy and my eyes a bit watery, but the earrings gleam in the light from the bathroom mirror. I like them mismatched. It means when they're finally matched, Rosa and I will be together again. It gives me hope.

I tell Sheryl the full story. She's shocked I've been allowed to keep the suite key but says she's glad I didn't tell her beforehand as she would have begged me not to go. It was too risky, and I could have gotten into a lot of trouble. But now it's done, she's all ears. I show her my gifts and she's so pleased for me.

"I wish I was young again so I could wear such pretty bathers," she says wistfully, looking down at her wide hips and rounded stomach.

Sheryl knows the international code for Australia, so we try Mum's phone. It doesn't work, no matter what we do. Maybe it's the same as the phones in the cabins. There must be some sort of communications blackout. I'm so disappointed—I realize I'd got my hopes up about talking to Dad too high. Especially today of all days, it would have been awesome to hear a familiar voice.

I tell Sheryl about the extra bedding and towels in our suite, and we try to work out why on earth that would be the case. It all seems so strange.

"Maybe they're expecting a big family group soon. But where would they come from? Who knows? We don't," says Sheryl.

"As if they'd tell us, and of course we can't ask, as that would give it away I've been there."

"I think it's best to keep it our secret for the time being, Jilda. Not even tell any of the other passengers. I think it would cause a lot of unrest, and people would be speculating even more than they are now."

Finally I go to bed, the bikini under my pillow and the earrings on the bedside table where I can see them as soon as I wake in the morning.

"Happy birthday, Jilda," says Sheryl softly into the darkness. "Sweet dreams."

Soon I feel tears seeping out of the corners of my eyes, running back into my hair. I gulp a couple of times, so I turn and burrow my face in my pillow, muffling the sounds so Sheryl won't hear me.

CHAPTER SIX
DAY FIVE SHIP

THE DAY starts in its usual monotonous way with our breakfast delivered. Room service is no fun here—it just means lack of freedom to us.

We spend the morning reading until finally, interminably later, lunch comes. At this rate, all we look forward to is dinner, and the chance to get out on the promenade deck for me to stretch my legs and Sheryl to get some air. But we are in for a surprise today. Soon after lunch the ship seems to stop. We can hear distant clangs, but the ship itself is still.

What on earth is going on now?

We are wondering whether we'll be allowed to take our promenade walk after dinner at all now the ship isn't moving. If we're in a port, perhaps they won't want us to see where we are.

Around three in the afternoon, there is an announcement over the loudspeakers to pack up all our gear and put our suitcases and other bags into the wardrobe. We're told we'll only have about thirty minutes to do this. After that we'll be called to the Vista Theater, and they say we have to bring anything of value, such as passports, credit cards, money, or jewelry with us. Sheryl and I look at each other in amazement and shock.

Are they going to rob us?

"I'm putting my money belt on," says Sheryl. "They'll have to physically undress me to get at my money and passport! I'm not letting anyone get their hands on my precious stuff."

I notice she takes off her wedding and engagement rings and puts them in her money belt too. She hikes up her skirt and fastens the money belt around her hips. She looks so incongruous with her large white undies hanging out in the breeze like that, but I've gotten used to seeing her in her underwear by now after so many days confined together.

I have a secure money holder that goes around my neck, so I get it out and check that my passport and money are in there. I don't have any credit cards yet, although I'm looking forward to the day when I will. Mum and Dad have both said we have to wait until we're eighteen for that. It's so annoying when they agree on something, as you know you don't have a chance to break their alliance. I guess it's kind of comforting they do stick together sometimes, though.

I wonder about Mum's and Rosa's important things. I've got their passports and Mum's phone from when I sneaked into our cabin, and Mum would have taken her credit cards with her for the day on their excursion in case of any unexpected purchases. I don't know whether to put their passports in with mine so they could all be stolen or leave them in the safe in Sheryl's and my cabin. I decide to keep theirs in the safe. I might get into trouble if I take them anyway, as they won't be expecting me to have Mum's and Rosa's passports. I lock them back up.

Sheryl and I pack our things. It only takes about fifteen minutes. Then we sit on our beds and speculate about what's going on. At last, a break in routine, and there must be some important news, or else they wouldn't summon us all together.

"They've definitely stopped, and so they must be letting us off, seeing as they've made us pack our bags," says Sheryl hopefully.

"I wonder where we are? I wonder if they've brought us back to Fiji?"

"No point letting us off anywhere if they steal all our valuables," says Sheryl. "How would we get on without our passports and credit cards?"

I've been wondering myself how Rosa and Mum have been going without their passports. Of course I've been secretly hoping that because they don't have their passports they'll still be in Fiji, and I envisage Mum and Rosa waiting anxiously but patiently on the pier for my return. But I know in my heart of hearts it's highly unlikely they'll still be there. It's so long since the ship left that port. And we probably won't be taken back to Fiji anyway, as that was what the man said right from the start.

Where are we?

Have we traveled around in circles for days, or have we traveled miles and miles across the seas to a distant land? We could have gone a long way in almost a week. Was it a week? I'd lost count of the days. It actually feels like I've been living on this ship for half of my life.

The announcement bell peals again, and we're told it's time to go. The guards at the end of the corridors take us via an internal route to the theater. I push Sheryl in her wheelchair, and when we arrive she insists we park her chair at the back. She hobbles down the stairs and we take a seat. We sit, crew and passengers alike, wondering what could be happening now.

Finally the man I spoke to in the empty auditorium on the first day of this nightmare picks up a microphone and begins to speak. He seems assured and excited now, not like the other day when he was shaking and nervous.

"This is the day we have been waiting for," he says. "From today, the rules on this ship will change. Since early this afternoon, many other passengers have been coming on board, and from now on you will be hot-bedding in your cabins."

"Hot-bedding, hot-bedding…." I can hear muttering all around me.

"What do you mean, hot-bedding?" Gavin calls out in a loud voice. His face is very red, and I worry about his blood pressure.

"What we mean is that you will all be allotted eight hours in your cabins. The end of each eight-hour interval will be signaled by the bell you normally hear before an announcement—but it will be three lots of the usual three so you can differentiate it from a normal announcement. The bells will be sounded ten minutes before the end of your turn in the cabin to give you time to collect what you need for the next sixteen hours."

The number sixteen is starting to sound like a very bad luck number to me by now. I've just had my sixteenth birthday on the ship of horrors, and now I have to stay *out* of my cabin for sixteen hours a day whether I want to or not. I'm beginning to think I never want to hear the number sixteen again.

"When your eight hours are up, this means you must stay away from your cabin until your scheduled time is due again. Use this time wisely for sleeping, as it will be difficult to find a place to have a rest anywhere else on the ship due to the numbers of passengers."

Everyone's starting to get really noisy.

"What about the crew? Does this include us?" asks a man in a tall chef's hat.

"You already work shifts, so now you will work eight hours, sleep eight hours in your cabin, and then return to work. Crew members, you will not be doing your normal duties. Most of you will now have to be involved with food preparation, serving, and cleaning up. We will soon be allocating you your new tasks."

"Oh, great!" calls another crew member. "Slave labor."

The man ignores the outburst and continues.

"As you will appreciate, passengers, dealing with such large numbers of people on board, we can no longer control where you go on the ship, but to keep things orderly, you must only go to your passenger deck, not wander around the other passenger decks. The public areas are where you can walk freely. You must abide by the rules of when you are allowed in your cabin. None of you can return to your own cabin for anything at all during the other sixteen hours, so you do not disturb the others sleeping there."

"What if we need to go to the toilet?" someone else calls out.

"There are plenty of public access toilets all around the ship which you can use. Your showers, of course, you will have to take during your eight hours allowed in your cabin. And keep the showers short. We have a desalination plant on board, but it will be hard for it to keep up with the volume of water needed."

"So, how many more passengers are you talking about?" pipes up a woman.

"I am not at liberty to tell you," says the man.

"Do the math. A full ship with three shifts means three times the usual number of people on board," I hear someone say behind me. Her voice carries as clear as a bell. I turn around to see it's the apple girl sitting right behind me. Her green eyes are bright and her cheeks flushed.

Hairs stand up on the back of my neck.

Gasps fill the theater.

I remember when we were reading about the ship before we came, we learned there were two thousand passengers and one thousand crew. That means the ship normally carries up to three thousand people. But with three shifts of hot-bedding, that means six thousand passengers can be housed on board.

But then I remember the extra mattresses I saw when I sneaked into our suite on my birthday. And the piles of towels. Maybe there will be even more people than we could imagine.

"You cannot go back to your cabins now. Other people are already settling in there. Your allotted time in your cabin is from midnight till 8:00 a.m. Count yourselves lucky your shift is the one with the most usual body-clock sleeping time, so make the most of it."

"So we're supposed to feel grateful now, are we?" says Gavin.

"Yes, you will be able to have the most normal routine of all shifts."

"What about meals?"

"All meals can now be taken in every one of the ship's restaurants and cafes again. Do not expect the specialty restaurants to serve exclusive food, though—each restaurant will be serving exactly the same type of food. There will be no more room service, as the crew numbers will obviously be very stretched—you will have just basic services. Some of the people coming on board will be helping with the food preparation, but there will continue to be no made beds, no bathrooms cleaned. You must do that yourselves to try and maintain some semblance of hygiene in your cabin. We must do everything we can to avoid an outbreak of gastroenteritis."

"That's all we need," I hear someone mutter.

"What about towels and sheets and pillowcases?" asks another. "Do you really expect us to sleep on strangers' sheets, and use each other's towels?"

"There will be enough towels, sheets, and pillowcases to have your own each. You will have fresh linen for your first shift, but after that there will be no more linen service. I suggest you put your sheets and pillowcases into your suitcases when you pack up your bed each day, or if there is not enough room in your bags, put your sheets inside your pillowcase and put them behind your suitcases for identification as yours. As for towels, drape them over your suitcases so they can dry out and not be used by somebody else. Towels will not be changed for the duration of the trip, so please look after them. No use dropping them on the floor expecting the housekeepers to remove them and provide you with new ones, as that will not be occurring. Of course, at the end of your shift, you also need to pack up all your toothbrushes, beauty products, brushes, razors, and so on, and keep the bathroom clear and safe for others to use."

"This is outrageous! You can't expect us to live like this."

"And how long will this go on for?"

"Approximately four or five days, maybe a bit more. About the same amount of time it took us to get here."

"And where is here?"

The man with the microphone looks across to a short, stout man dressed in a white shirt with a blue tie, who has been standing quietly at the side of the stage all during the speech. The man nods and comes over to the microphone.

"You will soon find out when you talk to the oncoming passengers, so it may as well be now. We are in the main port of Levy Archipelago."

More gasps.

I know where Levy Archipelago is. I've always loved geography at school. To think we've traveled so far! But then again we've been traveling day and night constantly for ages. Apart from that one time it felt like we stopped. Maybe that was when the extra mattresses, bedding, and towels were brought on board. And maybe more food supplies, or fuel....

"Why?" someone from the crowd cries.

"As you would have heard in the news over the past few years, negotiations have been continuing for a solution to the problem of rising sea waters inundating our islands. The sea level has risen so much that on high tides, and especially when a storm accompanies the high tide, the waters are flooding our houses. Many of us have moved to higher ground, but our islands are very low-lying. There is not enough land above sea level for all of our citizens to be comfortable and safe. Our fresh water is running out, as it is infiltrated with salt, and we can no longer grow our own food in the salty soil."

Sheryl grabs my hand and holds on tight. The man continues.

"Governments around the world have only ever agreed to take a certain number of us. But we want to stay together. We are one nation of peoples and we do not want to be split up to live in different countries. We want to be together as one group in one land."

The audience is quiet for a few moments as we take it all in. Then someone breaks the silence.

"How many citizens are you talking about, sir?"

"Approximately one hundred and twenty thousand."

"But how do you imagine you can get all of them off your islands?"

"Ships—including this one."

The theater erupts into noise. Shock and surprise fills the auditorium.

"How many ships?"

"Ten."

My God. Ten. Are nine other lots of passengers in a similar situation to us? But how can ten ships carry 120,000 people?

We've been out of contact with the world for almost five days, so we have no idea what has been in the news. The story of missing ships must be *huge* around the world.

But ten ships won't be enough for those vast numbers of people, surely. Somehow the maths doesn't add up.

"You will stay here in the theater until we leave port, ladies and gentlemen. It will not be too much longer and everyone will be on board. Thank you for your cooperation."

As I look back over my shoulder, to catch the eye of the girl behind me to see her reaction to what's happening, I notice the guards are blocking the exits in case any of us think of leaving.

Cooperation? Is that what they call this total lack of control over our own situation?

I turn toward the stage again.

"Why did you make us bring all our valuables with us, if you're keeping us on the ship? We thought we must be finally disembarking," I call out as loud as I can to be heard over the muttering crowd.

Sheryl squeezes my hand tighter and whispers, "Good girl."

"Because from now on you need to think about what you want to do with your valuables. Many people will be sharing your cabins at different times, strangers you have never met. Your cabins will no longer be locked, so you need to be as security conscious as you think you need to be. It will not be our responsibility if anything is stolen."

More mutters from the crowd.

"Great. That's all we need," grumbles Sheryl. "Thieves."

The ship lurches, and at last it seems we are underway once more.

Finally we're told we can leave. We begin to file out of the theater, the buzz of conversation deafening. I notice apple girl is limping up the stairs in front of us. But Sheryl is so slow, we can't keep up with her, and we have to collect Sheryl's wheelchair anyway.

Why do I care so much about catching up with her? Is it because I need to talk to someone my own age about all of this? Or is it because of her, who she is, herself?

But my thoughts about the girl are quickly pushed to the back of my mind, as we are surrounded by crowds of people as soon as we leave the theater. The reality hits me that there really are thousands more on the ship than there were before it was overtaken. It's slow going making our way through all the passengers, especially with the wheelchair, but most of them just move out of our way without saying a word. Many seem dazed and upset, and the atmosphere is strangely quiet considering the number of people around us.

We have to fill in our time until midnight. But, boy, is it ever a wonderful feeling to be so free on the ship again. We can go wherever we like, eat in any of the ten restaurants, swim in the pool, and best of all *not be stuck in the cabin all day*! Sheryl and I venture out onto one of the decks to see if we can see the islands we have just unknowingly visited. Large ships are scattered around the ocean, some not far away and others distant hazy images on the horizon. So many ships! Maybe they really *are* evacuating the entire population.

Already the land is just a few low humps in the ocean, with no distinguishing features from so far away. To think I've been there, in Levy Archipelago, and wasn't even aware of it. The whole time we've been kept in the theater, the ship was slipping farther and farther away from shore. And what really freaks me out is, the way they're talking, it won't be that many more years before the whole place is underwater and I'll *never* get to see it.

This is the first time the reality of rising sea levels actually hits me, and it hits me hard. I feel a lump in my throat as I watch the distant humps disappear over the horizon, knowing I will never, ever go there in my lifetime. That one day the islands won't be there at all. They'll be totally submerged.

I'm not the only one feeling emotional. As I look around me, I see people fixedly watching the land slip away. That is their home, and they're seeing it for the last time. Some are holding on to others as if trying to stay upright. Some sob loudly, while others wail. Many just stare, soundless.

I realize I've only ever thought about tropical islands as places to visit on vacation. Not as real people's homes. I've been living under a selfish first-world rock and feel ashamed.

After that gut-wrenching experience, I really want a swim. By chance we run into Gavin, who says he'll push Sheryl around for a while. I don't argue.

The pool looks tantalizingly clean, as no one has been swimming in it for days. Mounds of striped pool towels overflow from the towel-borrowing station, and there's not a towel attendant in sight. I presume they've had to take on other duties with the huge number of passengers now apparently on board. My bathers are back in the cabin, as we had no prior warning about our sudden shipboard freedom, but I'm wearing my good matching undies bought especially for the trip, so I think they won't look *too* different from a bikini. I'm not going to let that stop me going in after so long without a swim.

Pulling my dress and money holder quickly over my head in one go, I secrete my valuables in the crumpled folds of my dress on the deck. I wrap the towel around me so no one will have much of a chance to notice I'm in my knickers and bra rather than bathers. I walk to the edge of the pool and sit down. Quickly flicking off the towel, I slip in. Bliss!

I'm the only one in the pool, and it feels so good causing the first ripples to flow across its surface. Suddenly I'm deliriously happy on a day I've been so troubled. My mood has swung from dark despair to euphoria. For a few moments, I just feel free. Being out of the cabin and in the fresh air in the sun again—instead of only having our monitored evening promenade walks to look forward to.

The euphoria increases when the apple girl hobbles over to the pool and looks in. She obviously has the same idea and tears off her red T-shirt and pulls down her denim shorts in one quick move.

Wow! What a figure. She's got great legs and full boobs....

"It looks like I'm wearing a bikini, doesn't it?" she asks and, without waiting for an answer, hops in the deep end. When she surfaces, her long, curly brown hair is now pulled straight, hanging wet from her head. She flicks it over her left shoulder.

"Let's make the most of it before the hordes arrive," she says. She has a friendly smile, and I notice again that intriguing little gap between her top front teeth.

I've got a boyfriend. What the hell am I doing thinking a girl has a cute smile and a great body? Am I actually attracted to her?

I didn't know I could get attracted to girls....

We chat, speculating on what's happening. And we finally have a chance to introduce ourselves properly. Her name's Jade and she's from Kissimmee, which she tells me is in Florida. At first I think she's teasing me with a place name like that, but she assures me it's a real place and teaches me how to put the stress on the second syllable, not the first one, which I was doing when trying to repeat the name of her town. Her parents work for Disney World, which she says isn't that far away from their hometown. They, too, got off in Fiji for an excursion, while she stayed behind nursing a twisted ankle, which took several days to heal. That explains the lack of promenade walks and her current limp. I tell her about Mum and Dad and Rosa, but for some reason I just don't want to mention Zac. Not yet, anyway. I feel like his name would suddenly spoil this magic moment. I change the subject safely away from families and relationships and home.

"The pool will probably go downhill fast when all the new passengers find it. Let's enjoy it while it's as clear as it will ever be," I say.

"And hang on to our towels. I doubt we'll get another clean one again."

Even as we swim, more and more people come onto the pool deck. People of all ages—young parents or older siblings carrying babies, children through to teenagers, younger adults, the middle-aged, and the elderly. Some seem quite infirm and frail. Jade and I start to talk numbers. By the sound of it, there are about six thousand of us now, and considering there are some remaining crew members as well, the ship must be expected to carry even more than that. Unbelievable. But then I tell Jade about what I saw on my sneak trip to my family's suite. The extra two mattresses mean six people can be in our suite at the same time with two on the floor, two in the king-size bed and two on the sofa bed, and with three shifts it means eighteen people can be accommodated in that one cabin alone.

"I wonder if they're putting more mattresses in *all* the cabins?" speculates Jade.

"In that case, we're talking way more than six thousand passengers. Say they double the number that normally sleeps in each cabin by adding mattresses, like in my previous suite? Could we be going to carry twelve thousand? Plus the crew?"

"So at any one time, there would be four thousand in cabins or suites, and eight thousand wandering around! And as you say, there's the crew too."

"And he said ten ships. If they're all as big as this one, that's... that's... a total of more than one hundred and twenty thousand!"

We stare at each other in horror and amazement. The man said the population of Levy Archipelago is over 120,000. That's more or less the population of a third of Hobart. And on only ten ships. The weirdest thing about it all is that it's suddenly sounding just so possible.

The numbers are driving us crazy, so we just muck around in the water to take our minds off the brain-boggling figures popping around inside our heads.

Eventually, but reluctantly, I'm ready to get out. I swim to the edge and hoist myself up over the lip of the pool in one swoop. I'm so glad Mum bought us new underwear for the trip. I hadn't expected hundreds of people to witness me getting out of the pool in my undies, but that's what happens today.

I'm glad Jade's in the same situation as I am. I see the dark triangle through her wet lemon-yellow knickers as she pulls herself up over the pool edge, and quickly look away before she catches me. I drape the towel around me while I dry off a bit in the warm sun, put my money holder around my neck again, then slip my dress back over my head to look a bit more presentable. I don't feel *that* confident in my skin. Jade doesn't seem to be such a prude as I am and waits till her underwear is completely dry before tugging on her shorts, patting her pockets to check her valuables are still safely there, and pulling on her T-shirt. It gives me more of a chance to look at her.

I can't believe I'm checking out another girl's body. Rosa and I are comfortable sitting round in our underwear, but we're so used to each other and have done it since we were kids. Plus she's my sister. But looking at Jade is something very different. I try not to stare.

She sits and chats to me all the while, and I'm so happy to have someone almost my own age to talk to again.

But it's starting to feel like something else as well. Something I didn't expect to feel. Ever.

We promise to meet at the pool at the same time tomorrow, and I can't wait to get my new birthday bikini out of my bag and give it its first wearing. I really want her to see me in it. I think I want her to see me in it even more than I want Zac to.

Will she think I look good in it?

I hope she does. Suddenly I almost don't care about the scary situation we're in, as it's given me a chance to meet Jade.

Finally it's dinnertime, and the corridors are choked with people. All the restaurants are packed to overflowing, even though they put on two sittings in each restaurant. We only have a choice of two dishes for the main meal—either vegetarian or nonvegetarian—no starter, and dessert is just pieces of fruit. And I don't mean cut-up pieces of fruit either. I mean whole fruits like watermelon, rockmelon, pineapple, or papaya that we have to slice up ourselves unless we want something individual like an apple, mango, peach, or orange. There is a large jug of water and glasses on each table for us to help ourselves to.

After dinner we wander around, but it's like constantly walking through a crowd at the Saturday Salamanca Markets or at the showground on People's Day, being jostled all the time.

And Jade is still hobbling a bit, and nervous of people knocking her sore ankle.

Most of the new passengers look stunned and in total shock. Some are crying, some are angry, and some are just staring around in disbelief. None of them look like the happy tourists we all were when we first got on the boat, dressed in our holiday gear and posing for photos. Some still have their bags with them, as they haven't been allowed into their cabin yet, so many of them are just sitting on their luggage, heads in their hands, waiting. Parents try to pacify misbehaving children or crying babies.

We realize this is no pleasure cruise for these poor people. They have had to leave their homes, and for good. I can't imagine what it would be like to know that your island home is slowly drowning and that one day you'd have to leave. And now they finally have left. Did they feel forced to leave against their will, or did they accept the inevitable? Do they know where they're going? We certainly don't. I ask some of them, but they don't seem to know either. How could they have gotten on board not knowing their final destination? Or maybe that shows how desperate they are.

Jade and I finally go our separate ways after arranging to meet tomorrow. I'm so glad she wants to spend time with me again. I find Sheryl back outside our cabin at midnight, as the previous shift has just left, sitting calmly in her wheelchair. We've been separated ever since I went to the pool. Luckily Gavin had looked after her all day.

As soon as I open the door, I notice different odors. It doesn't smell like our cabin anymore. Other people have definitely been staying here in our absence. Four suitcases and some hand luggage that don't belong to us line the walls, with wet towels hanging over them. There is still steam on the bathroom mirror from a previous occupant's shower, and smatterings of talc cover the floor tiles. But they've cleared away all their personal items from the bathroom, as we also have been told to do.

Sheryl is shocked to find there are two extra mattresses on the floor, but I've been half expecting that. Our little oasis of privacy is gone, and our cabin is becoming remarkably cluttered due to all the luggage, towels, and bedding. I figure after the next shift comes in, there will be twelve bags plus assorted hand luggage in total. Sheryl's and my bags are still in the wardrobe where we'd left them, and we can still use the safe as only we know our password.

Soon another woman arrives to share our cabin. Her face falls when she sees us. This is the first time she's come to the cabin, so she has her luggage with her. She's horrified to see the mattresses on the floor.

We discuss who will be sleeping where. In our absence, the two king singles have been pushed together into one king-size bed to save floor space, and my bedside table has been repositioned. Stacks of clean bedding and fresh towels for our shift are there as promised, but we will have to make up our own beds. Upon closer inspection, we realize the sheets we have been given are one set of king-size sheets (so the beds will *have* to stay together now) and two single sets for the mattresses on the floor. Sheryl, being older and a bit incapacitated, really needs to sleep in a bed, but I can easily sleep on the floor. The trouble is, Sheryl says she feels uncomfortable having to share the bed with a stranger, and the young woman—who introduces herself as Simone—says she's happy to sleep on the floor. It seems our problem is solved. I'll sleep with Sheryl.

But when our next cabinmate arrives, with her worried-looking husband just behind her juggling all their gear, we realize there is no choice but to change sleeping arrangements.

The other woman to occupy our cabin is heavily pregnant, so she'll have to share with Sheryl—you can't expect her to lever herself down to the floor, and then it would be very difficult for her to get back up again. So we agree Simone and I will sleep on the mattresses on the floor.

"Come and lie down on the bed with me," says Sheryl kindly to the pregnant woman, whose husband has reluctantly left to find his own cabin he'll be sharing with other men on another floor. "You won't be lonely here."

After brief introductions, the pregnant woman, Marta, takes a pretty little pink shell from her pocket and places it lovingly on the bedside table on her side of the bed. I don't have the heart to tell her she'll have to pack it away tomorrow for when the next shift comes in and takes over our cabin. She carefully lowers herself onto the bed, one hand supporting the small of her back, then lies down and drifts off to sleep there and then. She must be exhausted from the strain of the day.

Trying to keep as quiet as possible so as not disturb Marta, we open our suitcases on our respective beds and mattresses and take out our nightwear and wash bags. We decide to leave our toothbrushes and other necessities on different parts of the bathroom basin and allocate rungs for the towels. At least that way they'll get a bit of a chance to dry off after our showers before we have to stash them away for the next shift. I suggest to Sheryl that when we have to leave the cabin, maybe she and I can hang our towels over the wardrobe door handles instead of over our cases, so at least they'll get aired, but not mixed up with the others' towels.

We can explain all the details to Marta in the morning.

All of this is really irritating, and I almost scream with frustration. But it isn't their fault, it isn't Sheryl's, and it isn't mine. All of these decisions have been made by the powers who have us in their control for the time being. I realize there will have to be very strict rules to ensure this huge number of passengers on board stay in some sort of order. And I feel sorry for the people who have had to leave their homes forever, with just a suitcase and small bag each. How unbearable it must be for them. How could you choose what to take from a lifetime of possessions?

We take turns having quick showers while Marta sleeps on, then finally all settle down for the night. We know we only have about six hours left now until we have to be up again, dressed and packed, ready for the next shift to move into our room. It is so weird sleeping with two strangers. Sheryl and I have almost become friends, or at the very least become very used to each other, and have kept each other good company during the previous confusing days. Now that everything is much more out in the open, it all makes more sense, but there is still a lot we don't know. Like where the hell are we all going? And what is going to happen to us after we get there? These thoughts swirl round and round inside my head, until finally the land of nod claims me once again—but my final thoughts before I fall asleep are of Jade climbing out of the pool, droplets of water sparkling on her skin.

CHAPTER SEVEN
DAY SIX SHIP

WHEN I push Sheryl to breakfast today, we talk about our new cabinmates. Sheryl appears concerned, saying, "That baby is going to be born any day now."

"You told me you were a midwife back in the days when you were working," I say.

"Yes, that's how I know it will be really soon, and that's why I'm so worried."

"But you'll know what to do, won't you? You can't have forgotten."

"I certainly *haven't* forgotten, which makes it worse. Things are far from ideal here to have a baby born into this situation. There should be a doctor on board, and maybe a nurse, as cruise ships are supposed to carry those in case of medical emergencies. But I don't expect they normally have to deliver babies on a cruise ship."

"Well, she's lucky she's got you on hand, then."

"Doesn't feel like luck to me," says Sheryl. "More like fate."

"Well, I think it's lucky you're on the same shift as she is. Imagine if she was on a different shift, sleeping with people who didn't have a clue what to do."

"It will keep me on edge, that's for sure," says Sheryl. "Even less chance of getting a decent night's sleep than before. And even *more* reason to hope this ship comes into a port soon, so she can have the baby ashore, somewhere with proper facilities."

I haven't noticed Sheryl having too much trouble sleeping. Once she puts her CPAP machine on, her regular breathing soon fills the cabin. But I don't think it's a good time to mention that. Nor to question why she would assume wherever we land will have a decent hospital.

"Should we do anything to prepare for the birth?" I ask, secretly hoping I won't have to be too involved. It all sounds quite scary really.

"We need to find out about the doctor, where she or he is, so we can quickly call them if the baby does start coming."

It is so weird at breakfast. I realize that with different shifts, passengers are on different time schedules. I just can't get my head around it. There are two groups roaming around the boat at any one time, while one shift sleeps. While we are ready for breakfast at 8:00 a.m., the next shift after us has gone to their cabins having presumably had their dinner at 6:00 a.m. or so (and how on earth could you be hungry for dinner so early in the morning?) and the other shift are hungry for... I'll really need to try and work it out.

I'm so glad Jade is an original passenger, so she's on the same shift as me. Yesterday, when we agreed to meet at the pool again, we didn't know if we would still see each other at meals. When we were by the pool, we hadn't really understood the full extent of the crowding. It will be impossible to be together at mealtimes now, unless we designate a spot to meet. Our friendship (*is that what this is?*) isn't at that stage yet, although I secretly hope it will be soon.

Finally it's time to meet Jade. When I got dressed this morning, I put on my new bikini under my clothes, looking forward to my swim later today. I hope she'll like my new bathers. I ask Simone at breakfast if she'll be so kind as to wheel Sheryl around for a while. I feel a bit guilty about that, but Simone readily agrees, as she probably thinks it's quite a burden on me having to do it all the time when we aren't even related. I say goodbye to Sheryl, who doesn't seem to mind that I'm abandoning her, and leave her with Simone.

But it's difficult to get to the edge of the pool today, as people are everywhere all over the deck. Sun lounges have six or more people sitting upright on them, three or four on either side. There is no way anyone would be selfish enough to lie down on one all by themselves, and even if they tried, I doubt other passengers needing a seat would allow them to stay there like that. The edge of the pool has people sitting squashed side by side, their feet dangling in the water to keep cool. The pool itself is just wall-to-wall people. You could only stand up in the water. You couldn't even do dog paddle.

This is freaky. I feel like we're human rats in an awful experiment. Everyone has lost their individuality, with so many of us trying to gain just a little space in the sun for ourselves.

I wonder about my towel. There's no way I'll be able to hang on to that. If I put it down, it will be quickly lost or taken. Well, who needs a pool towel? It's so hot, I'll just dry off immediately anyway—that is, if I'm lucky enough to even get into the pool to get wet.

Finally I spot Jade, who is on the opposite side of the pool. I can see she is scanning heads in the water, and I really hope that it's me she's looking for. Slowly I edge around, squeezing my way between people, until finally I'm beside her. She grabs my hand with relief. It feels strange. The skin on her hand is so much softer than Zac's, and her hand is much smaller. I can feel her fine bones beneath mine.

"I thought I wouldn't be able to find you," she says.

I'm amazed at the strength of passion in her voice. Perhaps all this weirdness has made her really appreciate a familiar face. But I hope it's more than that.

What is happening to me?

I squeeze her hand back. It feels so good to have a friend in among all this craziness.

"We won't get into the pool today, I don't think," I say. I'm disappointed about not being able to show off my new bikini, but I have to be realistic.

"I doubt it too. Unless they put the swimmers into shifts as well, but I guess they've got too much else to organize without that."

She gives me a cheeky grin.

I laugh. She's funny.

"Let's go look at the wake, then," I suggest. I know it will take us ages to get through all the crowds on the deck to the back of the boat, but I figure that will give us more time together anyway.

She holds my hand as we walk away from the pool, perhaps so we won't lose each other in the swirling sea of people. Maybe I can get used to this. Her hand feels so warm and reassuring, when everything else around us seems to be falling apart.

Jade isn't limping as much today, but we still make slow progress due to the crowds. When we finally get to the stern of the boat, we find a lot of others have the same idea, but at least we manage to get a spot on the rail and can lean out, looking at the wake and talking. It's quite noisy with the sound of the propellers and the wind, but we manage. We have to squash in really close together and speak into each other's ears to hear what the other is saying, and I'm really enjoying this feeling of intimacy. I can smell her shampoo on the breeze.

I could get used to this.

I like the way she holds my hair back with her soft fingers, so her mouth can get close to my ear without the wind flicking my hair into her face. I can sense her lips almost touching my earlobes, so I lean in closer to feel their feathery softness against my skin. I can feel her warm breath on my neck. My stomach flips around a bit, and I feel all weak inside. I don't think I've ever felt this kind of thrill with Zac.

I hold her hair back the same way when I answer her. I think I want more, but we're surrounded by people and there's no privacy. It's hard to concentrate on our conversation because I feel so strange, but I know we speculate about what our families are doing, and what's going to happen to us. I still don't mention Zac. It doesn't seem right somehow. Like it would spoil this special moment. We stay there for hours.

We're getting restless. It's now been six days we've been stuck on this ship with no chance to go on shore to stretch our legs or see new sights. All we've seen since we've been allowed out of our cabins is miles and miles of ocean and the far-distant, departing mounds of Levy Archipelago, and it's starting to get monotonous.

Starting to? Am I losing my mind?

It's been monotonous for days. The only thing now is Jade and I are beginning to develop a friendship, which helps. A lot.

When it's finally time for dinner, we go in together. Jade still holds on to my hand. I don't want to let go either. A few people stare down at our hands, then back up to our faces, but I can tell they don't know if we're just being friendly or if it's more. I don't even know myself. All I know is it's great to be able to continue to see her for a few more hours. We're seated at a table of about ten or twelve people, but it feels as if we're in a little private cocoon of our own.

Dinner over, we still have several hours to fill in until we can return to our cabins. We miss all the entertainment choices we had before but decide to go and look in the theater anyway. Perhaps we can find a seat there for a while if nothing else. It's hard having to stand up most of the day due to lack of seating space on the ship now that there are so many people on board, and Jade says her ankle gets sore having to be on it so much.

We make our way slowly through all the milling people, Jade laughing and walking just behind me, keeping her hands pressed lightly on my hips, so as not to be separated in the crowd. Her hands burn through my light cotton dress. As we wander through one of the bars, with a metal grill pulled down over the shelves lined with bottles of alcohol, she grabs my hand and drags me over toward a piano. She sits down on the piano stool and lifts the lid. I don't know what to expect, but she begins to play. Beautifully. People soon stop their conversations and crowd around her, transfixed by her spellbinding music. Her fingers fly over the keys. It's over as quickly as it started, and people begin clamoring for more. She plays another piece and the room is still. After she finishes there is a long silence, and then the clapping begins.

"More! More!"

Jade smiles up at me and puts the lid down.

"That was awesome," I say.

"Let's go," she replies.

We push our way through the crowds. Finally we arrive at the Vista Theater. When I open the door, we find we aren't the first to think of this idea. The theater is full of people, most of whom seem to be dozing in their seats. It's fairly quiet in here, as those speaking are trying to whisper so as not to disturb the sleepers. We find a spot on the steps and sit down on the floor, Jade behind me, grateful to find a place to rest our weary legs. We'd feel guilty taking a proper seat when so many of the passengers are older than us.

I can feel Jade's knees pressing onto either side of my shoulders, and then I feel her hands in my hair, her nails raking over my scalp. She tells me she is making me a french braid. Rosa and I often help each other with our hair. I love having someone taking care of me—it seems so long since I have experienced that. Zac never plays with my hair. I close my eyes and enjoy the sensation. My body tingles all over. Her clever fingers—piano and french braids. Jade is a total surprise.

Much sooner than I want, it's time to head back to our cabins for our sleep shift. Jade and I drag ourselves back up from the steps and leave the theater. I could have stayed there all night sitting with Jade and getting to know her better, but I know Sheryl will be worried if I don't come back to our cabin, and that wouldn't be fair to her.

We reluctantly say good night, looking at each other carefully. She takes a tentative step forward, and then I do too. Suddenly we're hugging, and I can feel her soft breasts pressing into mine. The smell of her sweetly scented hair takes my breath away. This seems so right. Different from Zac. Better. Warmer. I can't say anything—no words will come out of my thick throat. The world has changed for me.

We drop our arms, Jade smiling shyly at me, and we go our separate ways. As I wander back to my cabin, I am filled with such strange feelings, and I realize I'm shaking. I just don't know what's going on. I really like Jade and she seems to feel the same, but this is something I've never experienced before.

I've never felt so close to another female, not in this way. I wish I had Rosa to talk to about all the emotions surging through me right now. Although I'm not sure I could even find the right words to explain them.

Back in our cabin, reminded by Marta's huge stomach, I've soon got a distraction from my thoughts about Jade as I flick through the glossy folder full of information about the facilities on the ship. There is a doctor on board, as Sheryl had thought. But there's only a phone number to ring, which isn't much use to me, as the ship's phones haven't worked since we were first taken from the island. So I know we can't get any information that way.

I remind Sheryl we can't literally "call" the doctor, but that I will have to physically go and get him or her to come when the baby's arrival is imminent. I decide I'll need to go exploring tomorrow to find out where the "hospital" on the ship is, so we won't be caught out.

I tell Marta what I'm going to do, and her smile is warm and grateful. Our concern must be making her have increased confidence in us, as tonight when we're all lying in our beds and I ask her about her little shell, which she has yet again placed on her bedside table, she begins to talk about their old life on Levy Archipelago. Simone joins in with her own stories. We're starting to have an appreciation of what living there is like. They tell us of the years of worry as the tides have relentlessly risen, and all the changes that have happened to their islands because of that. The failed seawalls and sandbagging, the flooding houses, rusty cars, the salty-tasting drinking water, the damaged crops.

They reveal that many of the islanders had wanted to bring their animals with them when they were leaving, and how some had at first refused to go because they weren't allowed to take them. Apparently their belongings were carefully searched before they boarded, in case any small pets were being smuggled onto the ship. Both Marta and Simone are worried about the long-term fate of everyone's pets and livestock.

"The poor creatures," says Marta. "We've had to leave them all to drown. I keep thinking of the sea level rising and the animals clambering to higher ground until they have nowhere else to go. You know the highest point on our island is only about three meters above sea level."

We're all quiet as that fact sinks in.

Marta continues. "They'll all be squashed together in smaller and smaller areas and there won't be enough for them to eat, and the water will be lapping around their legs. It's such an unbearable thought."

I realize I haven't thought about that before—I've only thought about people being displaced by rising sea waters, and even that only superficially. It hasn't occurred to me to consider all the animals that will be affected too. At school, we talk about rising sea levels due to global warming, about crops being inundated and water becoming too saline to drink, and how people will have to move, but we've never once talked about what will happen to all the animals. It's now so obvious to me. They'll drown. I can't believe I've had such a simplistic view of the world before, and I feel like a veil is being lifted from my eyes as I listen to Marta and Simone talk about how important the animals are to the local islanders. They think it will be hard for many of the population to settle into a new life in a strange land without them, as they will be heartbroken knowing their fate.

When our conversation peters out and my cabin occupants seem to have finally drifted off to sleep, I find myself lying awake, thinking about the pitiful future awaiting the Levy Archipelago animals. It's just so distressing imagining what's going to happen to them back there. I try to distract myself from those awful images by recalling how it felt to hug Jade so tight. I've never felt so close to anyone before. Not even Zac or Rosa. It was different. More complete. And I want to feel it again.

Chapter Eight
Day Seven Ship

AFTER BREAKFAST, and with Sheryl safely in Simone's hands once more, I take the opportunity to go off in search of the doctor. I go to the information desk in the reception area of the ship first, seeing as the phones no longer work, but there is no one at the desk. Probably doing cooking or washing-up duties now instead. I decide to systematically search on every deck to see what I can suss out.

Of course I remember we've been told we're only allowed on our own sleeping deck or in public spaces, but they have long since given up trying to police that, due to the huge numbers of passengers milling about at all times of the day and night. No one would know who is supposed to be on what deck anymore—except it would be fairly obvious if men are walking around on a women's level or vice versa. The only rule that is really strictly enforced is having to get out of your cabin at the appointed time, as the next shift are there waiting outside the door, ready to come in and go to bed for their precious allotted time.

I don't think the hospital will be on any of the public entertainment decks, so I decide I'll leave them till last if I have no luck below. There are five decks of passenger cabins, from the ones with balconies like I'd shared with Mum and Rosa—I feel a lump in my throat when I think about that, but I can't stop and wallow in my own emotions, as it's too important to help Marta—through to cabins with windows (ocean view I think they're called) through to the interior ones like we're in now. They surely wouldn't put a clinic in a room with a balcony, or even one with a view, as they wouldn't care about giving patients somewhere to look outside, so I think I'll start right down in the bowels of the ship first.

Finally, after searching through several floors, I find an internal door that says Medical Center. At least it doesn't call itself "hospital," so that makes it seem less serious somehow.

I boldly walk in. The people in there are busy tending to an old man who seems to be having a heart attack or something like that. They either don't notice me or decide to ignore me as they have something so much more important to deal with than a nosy passenger. Or maybe they think I'm a relative of his coming to see how things are going.

I look around the room, and it seems to have a lot of equipment. It looks like the emergency department of a hospital. I've only been in emergency once, when Dad fell off a ladder and broke his arm, and we spent hours in there waiting for him to be attended to before finally getting help. There are heaps of machines that look to me like monitors of some sort, and maybe a defibrillator like I've seen in several locations around the promenade deck. There must be an awful lot of people on cruises who have heart problems, with so many defibrillators scattered around the place. Any wonder, with all the mounds of food passengers eat during a cruise. Before the ship was taken over, the amount of food some people had on their plates at the all-you-can-eat buffet was appalling. You'd think they couldn't go back for seconds. The worst part is, they probably did go back for seconds and have yet another pile. And then do the same with dessert. I'd noticed some passengers had two or even more helpings of dessert. Ugh! That's just plain greedy. With all the new passengers on board, the mood is quite different, and people only take what they really need to keep hunger at bay. Maybe some of them are so upset they don't feel like eating much anyway.

There are three beds in the medical center, and the man being tended to is lying on one of them. Finally one of the medical staff turns and notices me.

"What do you want?" she asks brusquely. I suppose she's pretty busy and doesn't want to have to deal with an unwanted intruder.

"I'm just trying to find out about this place."

"Why?" she asks. "Are you sick? If not, you'd better leave. You can see we're in the middle of an emergency."

"It's not me I'm here for. One of the women who's sharing our cabin looks like she's about to have her baby any day now. I was wondering what to do if the baby starts to come while we're still on the ship."

"That's all we need," she says sounding exasperated. "Women aren't supposed to come on board if they're more than twenty-four weeks pregnant."

"As if she had a choice," I snap back. "She's not a normal cruise passenger!"

I'm getting sick of her negative attitude, when all I'm doing is trying to get help for Marta.

If only Rosa could see me now.

She always puts people who are out of line back in their place straightaway. She's much braver than I am. I usually think of something I should have said as a comeback hours later, when it's too late.

"You're right. I shouldn't take it out on you, or her for that matter. When the time comes, bring her down here and we'll deal with it."

It. It. It's a baby coming, not an "it."

She turns her back to me and focuses all her attention on her patient once more. I can't wait to get out of here anyway. The old guy on the bed doesn't look too good.

But one of the nurses grabs me on the way out, shoving a pile of towels into my arms.

"You might need these," she says.

"What for?" I ask, feeling a bit stupid.

"For when the waters break," she explains. "And when the baby is coming."

"Oh," I say, not really understanding. I've never been around anyone having a baby before. I've heard of waters breaking, and talk of towels and hot water, but I'm not sure what all that entails. Sounds like I might be going to find out firsthand soon, whether I want to or not.

I leave the towels outside our cabin door as I can't go in, hoping no one will take them—I can't keep them with me all day. I wander around after that, until I meet Jade again at our now designated spot at the back of the ship looking out at the wake. I feel really close to her after our time together yesterday, but a little bit shy. I wish I knew what was really going on between us.

She's pleased when she sees I still have my french braid in, and rubs her hand down its length, giving it a gentle tug when she reaches the end. The hairs stand up on the back of my neck. She wonders how I've kept it so neat, or whether someone else has helped me plait another one. I admit I hadn't wanted to take it out, and that Sheryl had given me a tip to sleep with my shower cap on my head to stop it getting mussed up on the pillow. She said that's what she and her twin sister used to do to protect their "dos." Sheryl's tip has obviously worked. Jade laughs when I tell her what I've done—she thinks I would've looked hilarious lying on my mattress on the floor in my shower cap. Then I feel silly and think maybe I shouldn't have fessed up about that part. Maybe too much information?

But Jade quickly takes the heat off me by changing the subject and asking what I've been up to this morning. I fill her in about the medical center and Marta. We go for lunch, then spend the rest of the afternoon getting to know each other more. We have dinner together too, which, despite being surrounded by so many people as usual, feels like we are in our own private world. Sitting side by side at the table, I can feel her body heat, and can smell lemony soap on her skin. Sometimes she puts her hand on my knee and her palm burns on my bare skin. It leaves me feeling warm and shaky at the same time.

I finally wend my way back to our cabin, wishing Jade lived in Hobart, or even just in Tasmania, or even the mainland of Australia, as I know after all this mess is over, I'd really like to see her again. America is such a long way away, and Florida being on the east coast of the States is just about as far away as you can get from Hobart. I wonder whether she thinks about the fact that our real lives are normally so far apart.

If she does, does she care? I hope so. I really hope so.

When I get back to our cabin, I find the towels undisturbed beside the door, so I pick them up and take them in. Sheryl is flat on her back in bed, mouth slack, already soundly asleep and snoring. She's fallen asleep before switching her machine on and putting on her mask. I was right—it looks like Sheryl can sleep after all, despite being worried about the imminent birth. Marta lies next to her, belly huge in the bed, eyes wide open and staring at the ceiling. Simone lies on her side on her mattress on the floor, her face turned away from me. I can't tell if she's awake or asleep.

The night is not to be a peaceful one. In the very early hours of the morning, the baby starts to come, and there's no time to get Marta down to the medical center. I wake to the light being switched on and loud pants, gasps, and cries. Sheryl is already on her knees, head between Marta's legs. I hadn't realized Sheryl could be so agile, but maybe she just got into that position without thinking—on automatic pilot from her past life as a midwife. She had no choice but to do it. I can see some of those fresh towels the nurse gave me are already being put to use under Marta. Sheryl is muttering and encouraging Marta when to push and when not to, and how to breathe. Sometimes she tells Marta to pant.

"Go get the doctor," says Sheryl.

I don't need to be told twice. I can't wait to get out of the cabin with the strange smells, noises and atmosphere. I hurtle down flights of stairs until I reach the medical center's deck. I'm so glad I'd done my exploratory search before, as otherwise I would have wasted so much time searching for it deck by deck. The doctor is awake, despite it being the middle of the night. She looks drawn and exhausted. She sighs as she heaves herself out of her chair and follows me to our cabin.

Sheryl looks so relieved when the doctor arrives. The huge responsibility has been taken out of her hands.

The panting, followed by pushing, then resting, continues for quite some time, and I wonder how long it will all go on for. I ask Marta if she wants me to go and get her husband, but she says that in their culture giving birth only involves the women.

Finally, after quite a few hours, with a sudden rush, the baby slides out of Marta and onto the towels on the bed. I wait for the wail like you hear in movies after a baby is born, but the silence is eerie. The tiny little body lies still.

"Oh, no," whispers Sheryl.

"What's happening?" asks Marta, her voice worried. She too has been waiting for the cry of a healthy baby.

The doctor swiftly picks the baby up by the heels and whacks him sharply on the back—I can see the baby is a boy— but there is no response. She pokes around in the baby's mouth to remove some gunk to clear his airway, and then breathes very gently into his mouth while alternating with gently tapping his tiny chest with two fingertips. Still no response. The doctor then puts him over her shoulder. Nothing. The baby hangs limply. The little boy is blue. And he is so, so tiny and fragile-looking. He must have been born a bit too early, or there may have been something wrong with him.

The doctor carefully examines the baby, and then she and Sheryl deal with the cord. It isn't that much later that what I think must be the placenta flops out too. Sheryl tells me to get the plastic laundry bag to package up the mess. I feel like heaving, as I have to touch the placenta with my bare hands as, of course, there are no gloves for me to use. I dump it all in the bin in the bathroom, then scrub my hands furiously with soap and hot water, as hot as I can bear it.

What on earth are we going to do with the placenta long-term? We can't leave it in the bathroom for days on end. And what about the baby? He's clearly not alive.

When I come out of the bathroom, the doctor looks around at all of us and says, "We can leave the baby with the mother for an hour or so for bonding and mourning, but after that we must remove the body."

I think it's kind of the doctor to consider Marta's feelings, to give her time to spend with her baby before losing him forever. Maybe the doctor isn't as bad as she first appeared—perhaps she's just overwhelmed with all the sick cases she's dealing with, far more than she would on a normal cruise. It isn't just the sheer number of passengers—it would be that the new passengers taken on board are of all ages and in different states of health, with different medical needs. She must be so tired.

Sheryl has tears in her eyes as Marta reaches out to the doctor to take the baby and place him on her chest. My throat feels thick with emotion, and my stomach is tight.

Marta grabs my hand. "Please get my husband now," she begs. "Cabin 5074. His name is Jonas. He has brown—"

"Don't worry, I remember what he looks like from when you two first came to our cabin," I say, squeezing her hand, trying to reassure her.

I run to find his cabin and knock on the door. No response. I knock louder. It takes a while before a man in pajamas with rumpled hair, rubbing his sleepy eyes, answers the door. Jonas is right behind him and pushes past him into the corridor before I've even had a chance to say a word. He and I race back to my cabin. He rushes straight in and kneels beside the bed, one hand holding Marta's and the other stroking the tiny baby's head. The baby's sweet little feet are nestled in one of Marta's palms.

I wonder what they're going to do with the body of the baby, but we're soon to find out.

"We'll have to bury the baby at sea. A sea burial. I'm so sorry," the doctor says to Marta and Jonas. "We're not able to keep the baby's body on board for any length of time in this situation."

"A freezer," says Marta, her eyes imploring the doctor. "He can stay in a freezer."

Marta carefully strokes the baby's tiny, perfect fingers one by one, caressing the minute fingernails.

"I'm so sorry," repeats the doctor. "None of us really has any idea what's going on here, and what the end result of all this will be. It's best to have a service here on board. It will be more dignified that way—I'm sure you'd want that for your baby."

Marta looks deeply into Jonas's eyes, then nods her head. She can see the logic. They can't carry a dead baby around with them when they finally get off the ship, as who knows what awaits them, or exactly when that will be anyway. Or where.

The doctor stays with them for a time, then leaves, while the rest of us go out and stand in the corridor to give Marta and Jonas some privacy alone with their baby. We don't care who sees us in our pajamas.

CHAPTER NINE
DAY EIGHT SHIP

THE BABY'S burial takes place later this morning. When we have to leave our cabin for the next shift, I take the wrapped-up placenta, and soiled sheets and towels, and put them in my daypack to transport them to a waste disposal unit. I know I'll never use that daypack again, but I have to put the package in something to carry it safely. I don't want it to spill out of the plastic laundry bag in a corridor or on the deck. I have no idea what Sheryl and Marta will do for sheets now that their only set is soiled, but that thought is probably furthest from their minds at the moment. After I get rid of my sad cargo, I run up to the deck where I know the ceremony is to take place.

The doctor has wrapped the baby in a towel and secured the cloth with several large stitches. Marta holds the tiny bundle against her chest, her face pale, tears coursing down her cheeks. Jonas stands beside her, arm around her shoulders. He too has an ashen face. Marta takes the little pink shell from her pocket and tucks it gently into a fold in the baby's towel. It's an unbearable scene to watch. They must have had such high hopes for their baby and their new family, and now all that has been taken away. They would have no idea what their future holds.

The captain of the ship is to perform the burial ceremony. He wears his full ceremonial outfit, gold and brass sparkling in the sun, the whites of his clothes dazzling, his black shoes polished to a high shine. He looks utterly exhausted, dark rings under his eyes. I wonder how much sleep he's been able to get in the last few days. He says a few words, reading from a Bible, then encourages several people to step forward to lead the crowd in prayer. As the prayers fade away, a lone voice starts singing a mournful-sounding song, which is soon taken up by those who know the words. It must be in the local language of their country, as I can't understand what they're singing, but I can feel their sentiment. Everyone is somber, and many hold the palms of their right hands against their chests next to their hearts. People cry unashamedly, tears wet on their cheeks. Some openly sob.

Finally, the captain gently takes the wrapped-up baby from his mother's arms and puts the tiny body onto what looks like a large wooden chopping board. Maybe it is. Someone cries out, "Wait," and a man pushes his way through the gathered crowd, brandishing a small flag on a stick. He, or one of his family members, must have brought it with them in their luggage as one of their most treasured possessions when they had to leave their islands. The man holding the flag tugs hard to release the flag from its stick, and upon reaching the captain, drapes the little flag over the baby in the towel. It's a pitiful sight, but the flag makes the tiny bundle look so much more dignified.

The captain holds the wooden board with the baby's body resting on it over the side of the ship. The captain stands for a moment, arms outstretched, seemingly gazing at the horizon. Marta gasps and takes a step toward him, but her husband says, "Shh, shh," and pulls her back gently into his arms. She tries to tug away again, but as she does so the captain sighs deeply and slowly tips the board at an angle to let the parcel slide off, holding on to the flag by its corners with his index fingers. Looking over the side, I can see the towel-wrapped body fall, finally splashing into the ocean far below. It floats for a few moments, a minute package in the vast ocean. It quickly drifts behind us as the ship motors on relentlessly; then it dips beneath the white-crested waves. The baby is gone.

The captain gives the wooden board to a crew member next to him, then reverently folds up the small flag. With a nod from the man who had passed it to him, he gives it to Marta with two hands. She reaches out and receives the flag with two hands too. It seems such a dignified conclusion to the ceremony. She holds the flag to her chest as if she will never let it go. The crowd parts as she and her husband stumble away, clutching each other tightly, their eyes cast down, faces tortured.

After that, we have to fill in the day somehow until we can go back into our cabin. It seems everyone on that shift is aware of what happened this morning, whether they'd seen the burial ceremony or not, and people speak in whispers or stare out to sea, silent. The baby's death has affected all of us in different ways, and we realize we are alone on the ocean.

Even mealtimes are desultory affairs, with people queuing quietly at the buffet. Usually there's a bit of shoving and pushing, as passengers are becoming increasingly short-tempered with all they're having to put up with, but this tragedy has marked us all. We look at each other with a newfound respect. A life has been lost, a life that never had the chance to live. Who knows whether more lives will be lost on this cattle crate before we are freed from our confinement. I look around at my fellow passengers and see with fresh eyes just how vulnerable many of them seem. The old, the infirm, some with injuries they'd come on board with, several more pregnant women—anything could happen healthwise in this situation, and it will have to be dealt with here and now. Nobody is coming to rescue us. Nobody seems to know where we are. And none of us know where we are going or how long it will really take us to get there. Even though they said about four or five days, how do we know if that's true? And what will happen then?

I realize I have to try and stay positive, despite Marta's situation. I meet up with Jade, and even though I want to spend time with her, I tell her I really need to spend the rest of the day with poor Sheryl, who is beating herself up that she must have done something wrong, must have missed something, causing the baby to die. Marta and her husband Jonas had thanked Sheryl for her help, so it seems they aren't holding her responsible. Luckily, as she is blaming herself enough for something that wasn't her fault—something she worked so hard to help with, and it had all turned to tragedy. Jade squeezes my hand tight and tells me I'm so thoughtful. Nobody has ever said that to me before. I feel myself glowing under her praise. She says she understands, and to go to see Sheryl.

Marta has been taken down to the medical center to check everything is okay postbirth and is to stay there overnight, so that night our cabin seems eerily empty without her. I hop in with Sheryl in the king-size bed, sharing my single bed sheets with her as she no longer has any to use. We are a bit cozy due to the width of the sheets, but after our terrible day, I think we both appreciate feeling the warmth of another human being so close. I can't get out of my head the image of that little parcel slipping into the ocean, nor the feeling of Jade's hand gripping mine.

CHAPTER TEN
DAY NINE SHIP

WE'RE ABRUPTLY jolted from sleep by the ship pitching and tossing around. I've been dreaming of riding a horse, knees dug in tight to the horse's flank, and barely being able to hang on to the reins, so maybe that was the movement entering my consciousness before I fully woke to the reality. I almost roll off the bed onto the floor, and once I've switched on the light I can see Sheryl is hanging on to the bedhead for grim death, to stop her falling out of bed. Simone is sitting bolt upright on her mattress. Loud groans and moans seem to be coming from all around us, and from deep within the ship itself. It sounds like it's being wrenched apart by giant hands.

"What's going on?" says Sheryl, nervous.

"We must be in a storm," I say. "It's pretty wild. I'm going to go outside and have a look."

"Be careful, dearie," says Sheryl. I forgive her the "dearie" under the circumstances.

Normally I don't leave our cabin during our hot-bed shift, as I want to make the most of our limited time here, but I'm determined to see what's going on. And my stomach tells me I need fresh air, and fast. I've never felt this bad when we go sailing with Dad, but then again Mum always gives us some ginger tablets, with orders to chew them as soon as we get on board. But this sea is much rougher. I drag on my dressing gown and step out of the cabin.

It's really difficult walking along the corridor, and I'm weaving like I'm drunk to the eyeballs. My feet patter along almost without my control as the ship dips and leaps, and my stomach keeps flipping over. I find myself lurching from one side of the corridor to the other, so finally I hold on tight to the handrail on one side so I can walk a bit more steadily. Slowly I make my way to the end of the corridor and haul myself up the stairs, still hanging on to handrails. Other passengers are colliding with me or bumping into the walls with the motion of the ship.

Eventually I make it to an outside door. Rain pelts against the window set into the door, but I'm determined to go outside. I pull the door toward me to open it, and the force of the wind outside is so strong it almost knocks me back. Holding firmly with both hands and bracing my feet on the floor, I finally manage to hang on to the door as I step over the bulkhead to the deck. Then it takes all my strength to close the door again.

Water is sloshing around on the deck, and my bare feet are instantly cold, the bottom of my dressing gown sodden. Rain stings my face as the wind whips my hair around and flicks it into my eyes. The waves are gray, flecked with foam, and massive. It's too rough to go over to the railing, and anyway I'm worried I could be swept overboard if one of those huge dumpers decides to fling itself onto the deck. I breathe the salty air in deeply and will my stomach to settle. Finally I begin to feel a little less nauseous.

I can see hardly anyone else is out on the deck and think it's better to get back into the warmth and safety inside. But just as I'm about to open the deck door, I'm almost knocked over by someone coming out. It's Gavin, and he too can't sleep and feels a bit unwell. We huddle behind a pole, trying to find shelter from the wind.

"I wonder how much longer this is going on for," says Gavin.

"You mean the storm, or the whole thing?" I have to shout so he can hear me over the roaring wind.

"Everything. I don't think many of us can stand all the uncertainty much longer," he replies.

"I reckon we should approach the captain and demand answers."

"He won't just suddenly tell us, not after all this time of secrecy."

I know he's right. But we need to think outside the square.

"We could always tell him we'll throw him overboard unless he tells us where we're going. That way he'll have to spill the beans," I suggest.

"He won't buy that. And I don't think we would be threatening enough. He'll call our bluff, and we won't achieve anything."

We both look out to sea for a bit, feet planted wide while holding on tightly to the pole to keep our balance. We are mesmerized by the massive swell.

"I've got a better idea. Why don't you pretend you're going to throw *me* overboard?"

Gavin says, "I couldn't do it. I couldn't keep up the pretense."

"I could. I love acting. I've been in heaps of plays at school."

"I don't know, Jilda."

"Think about it, I'm serious," I say. "Anyway, I'm going in. I'm drenched and freezing."

I turn and Gavin helps me wrench open the door again, and I slip inside. Not being able to spend time on the deck means the interior of the ship is more crowded than usual, as people have to shelter somewhere. As I stagger back to the cabin, other passengers stare at my hair, which must be plastered to my scalp, and my dressing gown is so wet I'm dripping onto the carpet. Shivering, I enter our cabin and am grateful the bathroom is empty so I can have a hot shower straightaway to warm up.

While I'm in the shower, I'm surprised when Simone walks in on me. I'm just about to say something about privacy, but she rushes across the small room and leans over the toilet bowl, retching. I turn away so I don't have to watch as the vomit pours from her throat. Seasickness.

I feel a bit better after being out in the fresh air, but the sight of her throwing up makes my stomach turn again. Mum had stocked up on seasickness tablets for the trip, as she was worried we might feel ill, but none of us had needed any, as it had been fairly calm then. Now the conditions are quite different. The strength of my stomach toward seasickness has never been fully tested before on our day trips with Dad, his boat hugging the shoreline, and I'm now finding out that I don't cope all that well without at least ginger tablets.

Simone washes her teeth at the sink, apologizes to me, and leaves. The next minute, in staggers Sheryl, who does the same thing, grasping the edge of the toilet seat for support. It's getting like Pitt Street in the bathroom, and I have no time to be embarrassed that I'm naked in front of everyone. They are too busy throwing up to care anyway. Just as I'm drying off, in comes Simone again. I say nothing, just step aside and let her race to put her head over the toilet bowl. The sound of her vomiting turns my stomach even more. I've been prevented from hearing the other two puke sessions by the sound of the water in my ears in the shower. Now the sound fills the bathroom, and it isn't pleasant. The smell is saturating the air too, even though I have the fan on. I get out of the bathroom as quickly as I can, wrapped in my towel, and dress in the main part of the cabin. Up until now I've continued to get dressed in the bathroom, so I can enjoy a little privacy, but I can't stand the fetid atmosphere in there a moment longer. My head swirls, as does my stomach.

The others have lain back on their bed or mattress and are moaning softly. They look equally miserable. I notice they are pale, almost a gray-green. I probably don't look much different. At least if Marta's seasick, she's in the infirmary and can get looked after.

It's almost time for our shift to be over and to leave the cabin for the next sixteen hours, but I can see neither of them is in any state to move. But they have to, and they know it, because any minute now the next four passengers will be coming in to take our place. We still have to pack up our bedding, clear out the bathroom of our toiletries, and deal with our towels to leave the bathroom and beds free for the next shift. I feel sorry for them having to go into the puke-smelling bathroom, but there isn't much I can do. Then I have an idea. I return to the bathroom, tip some body shampoo down the toilet bowl, and swill it around with the toilet brush. It helps a bit. But the action of leaning over the bowl brings on a sudden retching that feels like it's emptying my insides out. When it's finally over, I clean my teeth and wash my face. I look at myself in the mirror. My face is white, but I feel a bit better now that I've spewed the contents of my stomach up at last. I squeeze out some more body shampoo into the toilet, but I hold the bottle at an angle and try not to look down and bring on another bout of throwing up.

I have to lever Sheryl out of bed and help her into her wheelchair. She says she's too weak to get dressed and doesn't care what others think of her out and about on the ship in her nightie, dressing gown, and slippers.

I strip the bed I shared last night with Sheryl and fold the sheets and Sheryl's pillowcase in a rough pile on top of Sheryl's suitcase. I put my pillowcase in my bag and Marta's on top of hers, and then deal with Simone's bedding. I'm concerned the identical towels, although we all have our special place to put them to distinguish them, have been indiscriminately grabbed to wipe mouths after the spew sessions, and I'm worried about the sharing of germs. But I'm determined not to let our hygiene standards slip, and I put our towels over respective suitcases and wardrobe door handles.

I find Sheryl's handbag and put it on her lap. She looks a total wreck and I can't take her out looking like that, so I grab her hairbrush from where I know she keeps it in her hand luggage and drag it several times through her hair. Now she looks much more respectable. Satisfied, I push her out into the corridor. The other four passengers are already waiting outside our door, looking seasick and miserable too. They look like they can't wait to get into "their" cabin and lie down.

It was difficult enough walking along the corridor on my own in the rough seas, but it's even more so pushing a wheelchair, although it does give me something to steady myself with. But it's hard going pushing against the strong forces that are working around us, and to make a clear pathway through all the people. Every now and again, when the ship pitches in the opposite direction, the wheelchair takes off on its own and I have to run along behind it, keeping up so it won't get away from me and crash into someone. It's much worse than the worst fully laden supermarket trolley with a crooked wheel I've ever had the misfortune to try and wrangle.

Finally, making our way through the crowds, and saying "Excuse me, excuse me," constantly, we reach the lifts. When the doors to the first one that arrives open, I'm braced to push Sheryl in, but realize immediately it would be impossible. The lift is so packed, there is barely room for one more person to squeeze in, let alone two including a wheelchair.

"Sorry," says one of the passengers who is trying to squash in farther to make space for us, realizing it's impossible.

I pull the wheelchair back, the doors close, and we wait for another lift. Same deal.

Finally, another one arrives which is almost as full. I fear we will be here all day. This time, though, a middle-aged man and two young women kindly get out of the lift to leave space for us.

"Thank you so much," Sheryl and I say simultaneously.

When we get to the breakfast room, I can tell, even though the room is crowded, it isn't as packed as usual. Perhaps a lot of other passengers are also being put off their food by the rough seas. Sheryl says she only wants a cup of coffee, but without her usual milk, and that she can't face eating anything. I tell her she needs to keep up her strength and that it's best to have something in her stomach if she feels nauseous, so it has something to work on. I force her to eat a couple of pieces of bread with honey. I don't spread on any butter as I think that might make it a bit greasy and turn her stomach again. Sheryl is fumbling in her handbag, and I ask her what she's looking for.

"Pills," she says. "I'm sure I had some motion sickness pills in here."

She gives up after a while and just sits there looking miserable. I realize I need to follow my own example and try and eat something too, even though I don't feel much like myself. The sight of a huge pile of strawberry yogurt in a large glass bowl makes me feel quite ill. I eat some dry bread and my stomach settles a bit. I think I should have a cup of tea, but the smell of it puts me off for the first time in my life. I just have a drink of water instead.

"I'll go to the infirmary and see if I can get you some seasickness tablets," I promise Sheryl. I can't stand seeing her looking so unwell.

"Finish your breakfast first," she says.

"I've had enough." I don't want to tell her I am fairly unwell myself, so I leave her sitting there and take off down to the medical center.

I'm not the first person there by far. A queue of people looking miserable, holding paper or plastic bags under their chins, streams out the door. Some of the bags look quite heavy and full. Ugh!

I give up on that and decide to go back to our original suite to get the travel sickness pills I know Mum has in her suitcase. I don't really want to disturb the people in there, but I've got little choice. I think about the possibility of taking all of my family's bags back with me to my cabin, but gathering them up and dragging them out would make so much noise and wake everyone up for sure. It would make our small cabin even more overcrowded too with all that extra luggage.

It doesn't take me long till I'm standing outside the suite door. I feel so sad looking at the number on the door, remembering once again how we'd been so excited the first time we found it. I knock gently to be polite, but there's no answer, so I try the door handle and it opens easily. I step into the room, which is quite dark, but there is a sliver of light coming from between the curtains that lead to the deck. It's just enough for me to see the wardrobe, although I have a strong recollection of exactly where it is anyway. I open the wardrobe door and feel inside. I hope I won't wake any of the passengers now, as they'll think I'm a thief sneaking around in "their" cabin. I can hear the soft purrs of a couple of the sleepers and then a louder snore.

I know Mum's bag has a long, plaited ribbon that looks like a colorful braid tied to the handle. She'd wanted something distinctive, so she could easily find her bag on a baggage carousel in among hundreds of similar-looking items of luggage. The first bag I touch doesn't have anything attached to the handle, so I fumble across to the next one. I feel the familiar satin of the plaited ribbon, and tears spark into my eyes unexpectedly. I remember Mum sitting at the kitchen table in Hobart, several lengths of differently colored ribbon in front of her as she plaited her ribbon into a cord. She made ones for us too, using a different combination of ribbon colors. Much more distinctive than all the tartan ribbons passengers think make their luggage look different from the others. I mean, I know there are lots of different tartans, but how well did people really know the pattern of the tartan they had chosen when so many other cases also sported tartan ribbons? I hope this is Mum's bag and not Rosa's, as I don't think Rosa has seasickness pills too. Mum had taken care of the medical stuff for all three of us. I drag out the case onto the carpet and as I do, the snorer makes an abrupt snort.

Oh no, one of them is going to wake up!

I don't really want to have to explain what I'm doing here. I don't want them to know who the strangers' bags in their cabin belong too, either, for some reason.

85

The sleeper seems to roll over, and then settles back into a steady snore. Maybe I'm going to get away with it.

I pull the suitcase open and fumble around inside. I wish I'd thought to bring my torch, although that would probably have disturbed the sleepers anyway.

My fingers touch objects that are hard to tell apart. Shoes are easy, but the clothes are not. Nothing there, so I decide to zip open an outside pocket on the case. The sound of this zip seems even louder than the main zip, and I don't know whether to pull it open slowly and drag out the noise but keep it quieter, or zip it open quickly and get it over and done with. I decide on the slow and quiet method. I don't want to get sprung now that I'm almost finished in here. It seems to take forever, with a quiet rasp now and again as the zip gets caught as it slides along. Finally I get the outside pocket open, and feeling around, clasp a small box. I can feel it has raised dots on it and I remember noticing there were Braille dots on the package when Mum bought them. So I'm pretty sure this is what I'm after. I remember she'd bought several packets, though, and I think she had bound them together with a rubber band, but I can't find anything like that and I don't want to spend any longer in the room than I have to and get sprung.

I close the pocket and the suitcase and slide it back into the wardrobe. When I get out into the light of the corridor, I open my fist to see what's in it and am surprised to find it's a packet of pills, but not what I'm looking for. It's a packet of *the* Pill. Was that Mum's suitcase I had been looking in, or Rosa's? I didn't know Rosa was on the Pill, and I thought I knew everything about her. Or are they Mum's, and why does she need them? She and Dad have been divorced for years. I feel really strange not knowing such an important fact. I don't want to go back in again to try to find the seasickness tablet packets, as I've risked being caught enough. I'll have another go at the medical center to see if I can get some travel sickness pills there.

When I arrive the queue has shortened, so I join it and try to relax, breathing deeply to keep the nausea down. Finally it's my turn, and I ask for some motion sickness pills. The nurse gives some to me but says, "Don't take too many at once. Just have the bare minimum to keep the sickness at bay. We only have a limited supply, and they're nearly all gone."

I take them gratefully and return to Sheryl, telling her we need to ration them carefully.

But I know I need to get back into my old suite again some time, to get more pills. Next time I'll take my torch, so I can be sure which bag I'm looking into.

As the day progresses, the weather does not abate. It's becoming putrid walking round the ship, as there are piles of vomit everywhere. Crew members are being dragged away from their food preparation duties (well, not as many people would feel like eating anyway, I suppose, if they're so sick) to clean up the mess. I feel sorry for them, as some of them are heaving as they do so. They aren't trained to do this, so it would be foul. I should volunteer to help, but I don't want to tip the balance of me feeling almost okay now that the seasickness tablets have finally kicked in. I know if I start to get up close and personal with piles of puke, that maybe it won't take too long until I'm adding to it.

I decide the best time to get into my old suite is between shifts—being up-front about what I'm doing is probably better than sneaking in while people are asleep, as they might get agitated and grab me, thinking I'm a robber. Those people who came on board have so few possessions, as all that is most important from their old lives must be in their suitcases, unlike we original cruise passengers who only have our cruise requirements with us. They might have precious photos, documents, money, or even jewelry with them that they'll be stressed about keeping safe.

I can't get my head around the fact that they all came on board, not knowing where they were going. I know we original passengers have been kept in the dark from the beginning so we can't say anything and cause unrest, but the others, and there seems to be thousands of them if my maths stacks up, tell us they'd just been told to pack their most precious possessions in one suitcase and a small bag each, and when they got on the ship they had no idea where they were going. They were told the secrecy was essential, as their government didn't want word to get out to the rest of the world about where they were heading, until it was too late to be turned back. I suppose you can't trust at least a few among thousands of people not to spill the beans and ruin the surprise element.

I'm amazed they seem so stoic about not knowing where they're headed, but I think they've had years to come to accept that they can no longer live on their islands, as the flooding from the sea-level rise is unabating. And they'd have to place their trust in their leaders that they will be taken somewhere suitable. All they know is they're leaving their island country forever, as it's drowning in the rising seas, and they have no real choice. I suppose any home would be better than no home, as long as you know you'll all be staying together.

So, at the end of that eight-hour period, I boldly walk to the door of our old suite and wait with the next shift outside the door for the previous shift to come out of the cabin. I explain to those waiting what I'm doing, and they seem fine with it, although one of the women looks a little stressed, eyes darting back and forth. She eventually assures me it's okay, as they are my family's bags, after all.

"Why don't you just take the bags with you?" another woman suggests. "It will give us much more room in our cabin and save you having to come back again."

The agitated woman doesn't appear so happy about that, but she looks like she doesn't want to make a fuss in front of the others. She casts her eyes down to the floor, avoiding all eye contact.

"Okay. Cool. Suits me," I say.

Even though I think that maybe those I'm sharing with won't appreciate the extra gear clogging up the space, I owe it to Mum and Rosa to have their cases safely under my watch, rather than in with a group of strangers. And the agitated woman is making me feel suspicious.

When the leaving shift comes out, I also explain to them what I'm doing. They believe my story, and I think they're pleased I'm making more room for them and their gear, so they have no objections. I go in with the current shift, and first of all I ask if I can open the safe. They haven't been able to use it anyway, because it has our code in it, so they don't mind—none of their treasures are stashed in there. I pull out the wads of paperwork Mum had put there, and stuff it into her hand luggage bag. One of the women helps me drag the cases and hand luggage out into the corridor. I balance one piece of hand luggage on top of each suitcase to make it easier. I don't want to leave one case behind while I roll the first one to my cabin, so I struggle along, pulling both of them topped with hand luggage behind me, one suitcase handle in each hand.

Suddenly the agitated woman is by my side.

"Can I help you take the bags back to your cabin?" she offers.

She seems to have settled down a bit, and at first I say no, but she insists, so I let her. I'm grateful for her help, as it will take me a long time to get back all by myself juggling so many bags. We don't talk much on the way.

When we arrive at my cabin door, I thank the woman and she heads off in the direction we came from. Then I realize I can't take the bags in, as the third shift has already taken possession of our suite. I wish I'd thought it through more, but it seemed such a good opportunity at the time. I decide to sit on one of the bags and keep an eye on them all, but I know the next almost eight hours are going to be awfully tedious. I've missed out on lunch, not that it really bothers me with my iffy stomach. More importantly, I've missed my appointment with Jade.

What will she think of me? I hope I don't blow it with her.

She'd understood I had to spend time with Sheryl yesterday, but I hadn't turned up to explain why I couldn't spend time with her again today. She'll think I'm unreliable, and I don't want her thinking that. I hope she'll understand when I finally get to explain it all to her, that I couldn't leave my family's bags unattended in case something happens to them. So to fill in some time, I open up Mum's case first—I can easily recognize which are her plaited ribbon colors, as distinct from Rosa's, in the brightly lit corridor—and rifle through her things.

I find the packets of seasickness tablets held together with a rubber band as I had remembered in one of her suitcase pockets, and also find some other things I think might prove useful. Mum always makes such a fuss about hygiene and had brought a dozen small bottles of hand sanitizer on the trip, even though we heard it was to be supplied on the ship. She wanted to have her own personal supply, for when we were on shore for excursions, or at airports or wherever. She was really pleased to see the large hand-wash dispensers scattered around the ship, at the entrance to the restaurants and theaters and near the lifts. But I've noticed lately they're pretty much empty, and though at first they were replenished regularly, supplies are probably rapidly running out due to the huge numbers of people swarming around the ship.

Mum has about a dozen little packets of tissues too (Mum loves buying things by the dozen) in another pocket, as well as a first aid kit stocked with Band-Aids, antiseptic cream, antidiarrhea tablets, some antibiotics, plus a few other packets of things. It makes me think the Pill packet I got from an outside pocket must have been from Rosa's bag. I can't wait to see Rosa again to find out what she's up to. How can she be on the Pill without me knowing? I thought I knew everything about her. Maybe her relationship with Andy is more serious than mine with Zac? I'd never questioned it before.

Going through Mum's stuff brings tears to my eyes. She'd been planning for the trip for months and had taken us on several fun shopping trips to buy clothes suitable for a cruise. There are a couple of colorful sarongs and a pair of bathers, strappy sandals, and several sundresses. She'd even bought herself some new underwear too. That makes me realize my supply of clean clothes is starting to run out. In the last few days it's been almost impossible to do any handwashing, as there are no empty rails to hang things on in the bathroom with so many of us sharing, and no spare clothes hangers to use. There is certainly no laundry service anymore. I don't really want to wear Mum's clothes, as I've never done that before, but I know Rosa won't mind. I feel bad that Rosa hasn't had a chance to open her birthday presents—hers are still safely snuggled in Mum's bag—whereas I had a chance to open mine on the actual day.

I'm so glad Mum's bag doesn't seem to have been tampered with. Seeing as there are so many people staying in our old suite at different times, it appears all the newcomers have respected the privacy of the people who own the bags that were there before they arrived to take over the cabin.

So I open Rosa's suitcase, hoping for the same. Now I really start to choke up. I hold each item of clothing or underwear up high and look at it as if it's the first time I've ever seen it. They all scream of a teenager going on a fun cruise, and look at the disaster it's turned out to be. Her sarongs are so pretty and floaty, and her bathers barely worn. Even her new flip-flops are hardly dirty or scratched on the bottom, they've had so little wear.

I zip open the outside pocket of Rosa's bag, the one I suspect is where the packet of the Pill had been hidden. I take the packet out of my pocket and put it back where I'd found it. I have a scrummage round to see what else is there. Down in the bottom I find a small, soft black drawstring bag. This isn't Rosa's, I don't think, but then again I'm starting to wonder what I know about Rosa if she's on the Pill and I don't know anything about it.

I carefully pull the drawstring open and tip out a pretty sapphire and diamond ring into the palm of my hand—well, it looks blue like a sapphire and sparkly like diamonds to me. Now I know for sure it isn't Rosa's. It can't be. I know all of Rosa's jewelry intimately, down to the last earring that has lost its mate that she can't bear to throw out. All our jewelry is costume jewelry. Unless Andy had given it to her and she didn't want me and Mum to know about it yet…. Maybe it's her sixteenth birthday present that he gave her before we came on the cruise? Zac didn't give me anything to open on the day….

I just don't know anymore. I think back to the agitated woman who helped me with the bags and wonder whether she knows something about the ring. No wonder she was so interested in helping me. She probably wanted to know which cabin I was taking the cases to. Is the jewelry hers? Was she making sure it wasn't stolen from her, by hiding it in someone else's bag? Or had she stolen it, and was hiding it in another person's bag who she knew wasn't on the boat anymore and therefore wouldn't be looking in it?

Anything could happen on a cruise ship overcrowded with passengers. I don't know what to do. If it's Rosa's, I have to make sure it isn't lost or stolen. If that woman has stolen the ring and hidden it in Rosa's bag for safekeeping, she doesn't deserve to have it returned. But if it is hers and she's trying to hide it from prying eyes, she has to get it back. Maybe the packet of the Pill is hers too? I decide it's best not to overreact, and to think about it for a while. I really need to talk to Sheryl—maybe she'll have some sensible advice.

I eventually need to go to the toilet, so I have to leave the cases in the corridor and hope nobody will rifle through them in the short time I plan to be away. I thread the ring onto Rosa's chain, together with her charm I've been wearing around my neck constantly since that first day I had to leave the cabin. That will be the best place for it, whoever it belongs to. I push the little bag that had contained the ring back into the pocket on Rosa's bag. I don't feel I should leave such a valuable-looking ring that doesn't belong to me in the corridor where somebody else has the opportunity to take it. It makes me realize how lucky I am that with the eleven other people I'm sharing the cabin with through all of the three shifts, none of our gear appears to have been touched, which surely means they are an honest group of people. But you can't trust everyone, I know that. With the number of passengers on board, there is bound to be the odd opportunistic thief or two.

While I'm away, I decide I'd better have something for dinner to keep my stomach lined. I go to the bistro and grab a couple of pieces of bread and slam some cheese slices between them and palm an apple as well. I look around for Jade but can't see her in the crowds. She's probably gone to the restaurant we've been to before, anyway. I hope she won't be too upset with me that I didn't meet her at the ship's wake that afternoon and will understand my reasons when I get the chance to tell her.

When I return to our cabin, the cases are packed neatly where I left them, but the outside zip pocket on Rosa's case hasn't been completely closed. I thought I'd zipped it up fully before I went to the toilet and then the bistro, but I can't really be sure—maybe I had left it slightly open. Or maybe that woman had come back while I was away. I'll really have to start taking more notice of things, I decide. I rifle through the pocket, and then the rest of the bags in case I've confused where I put it, but I can't find the little black jewelry bag anywhere. It's gone! And so has the packet of the Pill. There's nothing I can do for the time being, and I still have the ring safely in my possession around my neck.

I zip the bags up fully again, even though I know that won't make any difference—it just makes me feel more secure for some reason. I sit on Rosa's case, lean my head on the palm of my right hand, and with the fingers on my left hand I drag the ring and charm along the chain, back and forth, back and forth, and think.

What am I to do about this? Tell the captain there might be a thief on board? But what good will that do?

Will the woman—it must be her from our old cabin; who else could it be who would know to come looking for the ring—come back to try to claim it? Eventually my head feels heavy and I drift off, trying to sit upright on the case, as the ship is still pitching wildly around.

I'm jerked awake with a particularly violent thump, nearly losing my balance on the suitcase. I can hear the ship groaning and straining against the wild ocean. I hate to think how many of the passengers will now be sick with the motion and am so glad of my backup supply of Mum's pills.

Finally Simone comes along the corridor, pushing Sheryl, with Marta not far behind them, ready for our shift in the cabin. Marta has been pronounced fit to leave the medical center. Simone and Marta look surprised that I have more suitcases plus hand luggage with me to cram into our room, but they fully understand once I explain it all to them. Now that Sheryl has seen me with my family's luggage, she wants to make sure she has her sister's safe too and asks if I'll help her get it sometime soon.

While we're waiting for the other shift to come out of our cabin, I show them what is hanging around my neck on my chain. I explain how I found the ring in Rosa's case, and that the jewelry bag it was in, and the Pill packet, have been taken from the case while I was away.

Sheryl in particular seems worried.

"You know the ring most likely isn't your sister's, or mother's, so it certainly belongs to someone else. But why would they put it in your sister's bag?"

We decide it must belong to that woman from my old suite, who was trying to hide it from prying eyes, as otherwise how would it have gotten there, and who else would have known to look in the bag and take exactly those two things that don't belong there?

I slip the ring off the chain, and Simone and Marta have a good look at it, holding it to the light and twisting it around and around. They agree they are pretty certain it looks like the blue stone called lucretia that is only found on their islands, so it must come from there. They don't recognize the ring itself but say it would be expensive, as the stone is rare. All three women decide the other stones are diamonds too. So at least I was right about the diamond part. I realize now it really can't be a ring Andy gave Rosa. He wouldn't be able to afford to buy such a unique stone.

"I reckon the person who owns it must be hiding it from the others in their cabin," I say. "Maybe it belongs legitimately to someone there, but if that's the case, they would've told me when I took the cases away—although I didn't speak to anyone on the third shift, only the ones going in and leaving at that time, so I only covered two shifts. And neither shift I spoke to asked to get it out, so if it wasn't theirs, it was someone on the third shift, legitimately owned or not, or someone hiding stuff in the shifts I spoke to."

It's getting so complicated trying to explain what I'm thinking, and I know what I said came out all muddled. And I feel bad calling people "shifts," but it's the easiest way to say it.

"Let's hope there's not a thief on board, but statistically, with just so many people, there would have to be several thieves at least I'd say," says Sheryl, echoing my previous thoughts. "If not worse…."

"Yes, I agree. But what do you think I should do with the ring? The woman must've been very upset when it wasn't in the little black jewelry bag."

"I think if the ring genuinely belongs to the woman, she would have been open with you about it from the start," says Sheryl. "Even if she hadn't wanted her cabinmates to know about it and was hiding it from them, she could still have spoken to you when she was helping you bring the bags here."

I thread the ring back onto Rosa's chain for safekeeping.

"Maybe she didn't want me to know about it either."

"Perhaps you should put a note under the door of the suite, even a separate note for each shift in case the first note goes missing between shifts, saying you found something in your sister's bag, without saying what it is, and see if anyone contacts you to claim it. I don't think you should approach any of them on your own, but if you give a time to meet at this cabin, I'll be with you—you won't have to deal with this alone."

"Thanks so much, Sheryl. I'd be nervous to go back again on my own, as now I don't know whether all those people in that suite, especially that one particular woman who helped me with the bags, are trustworthy. But I could slip three notes under the door at different times, when they're in there sleeping."

"And if someone does come to our door, don't tell them what you found—let them tell you. That way we'll know they aren't just pretending. And we can ask them why they put both things in this bag rather than their own, so at least they'll have to explain it. We should be able to tell if they look nervous or embarrassed."

"What would I do without you, Sheryl? I can't just keep the ring—I really want it to go back to its rightful owner. I just don't think it's that woman who helped me, though."

"You're a good, honest girl, Jilda," says Sheryl. "Your parents should be so proud of you."

Wow! Sheryl thinks I'm honest, Jade thinks I'm thoughtful. I didn't realize those things about myself.

I'm pleased Sheryl thinks that about me. But her comment reminds me of Mum and Dad, not that I need much reminding, and I feel lost and lonely again. I wonder what they think has happened to me. They must be worried sick—at least I know I'm alive, fed, and so far safe, even if a bit spewy, but they won't have a clue where I am or what situation I'm in. I hope we can all find some peace and answers soon.

The shift comes to an end, and as that lot of passengers come out of our cabin—I must say, also looking fairly green—finally I'm free to enter, as it's our turn to be in there once again. I stash the bags under mine and Sheryl's after I ask her if that's okay. Otherwise, if I have to keep them all under my case, the stack would be ridiculously high and probably topple over. Luckily, Sheryl doesn't seem to be in too much of a rush to get her sister's bags as well, as it would get completely out of control. I keep the necklace with the ring on it around my neck. Will someone creep in during the night while we're asleep, looking for it?

CHAPTER ELEVEN
DAY TEN SHIP

DURING THE night, one by one my cabinmates complain of diarrhea as they have to continually rush to the bathroom. They keep me awake half the night—if it isn't one of them it's another. Fortunately, I don't seem to have caught that particular bug. Cross fingers. I'm so grateful for Mum's first-aid stash, because as soon as I have the first sign, I'll take some of her antidiarrhea tablets to stave it off. Meanwhile, I give some to Sheryl, Marta, and Simone. They thank me profusely, gulping the pills down, and eventually their dashes to the loo slow, then cease altogether.

Before we leave our cabin for the day, I squirt some body shampoo down the toilet again to try to clean it, as it has become foul so quickly. At least I don't throw up when I'm bent over the bowl this time, although I have to fight against it. I'm worried about what we'll find when we return in sixteen hours for our next shift in the cabin, as the other inhabitants might be ill as well. Seeing as the diarrhea pills seem so effective, I decide I need to share my limited supplies with those on the other shifts in our cabin too, or it will become completely uninhabitable.

I give a packet to the shift coming in after us in case they need it, and then duck off to my old suite to leave the note there about the item I found in the suitcase. I know I will have to go there again for the next shift to leave another note, and also go back to my current cabin to give the next shift a packet of antidiarrhea tablets too. At least our groups in our cabin can hopefully stay well. As for those on the rest of the ship, I'm afraid it has to be every person for themself. My few packets of tablets can't help the thousands on board, and it soon becomes clear this disease has pretty much spread throughout the whole ship. If those in our cabin stay healthy, we can be of some use to others.

As the day goes on, it appears the vomiting is getting worse, and it seems more and more people begin to get diarrhea as well. It's much more than seasickness. Sure, the weather is rough and the seas high, but that won't give you diarrhea.

I've heard of an illness called norovirus, or something like that, that passengers on cruise ships sometimes get due to lack of hygiene, which is why they have so many huge hand-sanitizer dispensers around the ship. But I've noticed they must have finally run out of supplies. I'm once again so glad of Mum's fixation with hygiene, as I've been using her little bottles and sharing them with my cabinmates.

I manage to make it to our meeting place at the back of the ship today and am relieved to see Jade is already there waiting for me. She says she's been worried about me, not having seen me for a couple of days. Jade seems to be bearing up pretty well healthwise, but we don't know how long that will last, so I give her some tablets in case she starts feeling ill. Jade suggests we go to the medical center to offer some help, as she says she feels useless just sitting round doing nothing much when there are so many people in need of assistance. I agree, even though I'm not sure how I'll cope, as I really want to spend more time with Jade.

The nurse says she's happy to take up our offer, as she's overwhelmed with sick people and the medical center's supplies of medicine have almost run out. She puts us to work cleaning people up, helping them to the bathroom, rinsing out their befouled clothes and ugh, ugh, ugh. It's horrible, but at least I feel I'm contributing, and the bonus is I get to stay in Jade's company. I'm impressed with how calm and efficient she is with everyone. Nothing seems to faze her, and she has a smile and kind word for everyone. I'm really getting to like her.

We stay with the nurse until we're dropping and ready for bed. The only break I've had from the medical center was in the afternoon when I raced back to my cabin to give tablets to the next shift, and my old suite to slip yet another note under the door for their next shift. I feel like all I've been doing is running. It's time for our shift in the cabin anyway, and if I don't sleep now, I won't be able to for another who-knows-how-many hours (this shift stuff is really hard to keep your head around) and I won't be of use to anyone if I'm totally exhausted.

Outside the medical center, Jade and I give each other a high five of success for our work that day, then stop and really look at each other. A few seconds beat by. Our eyes lock. I look away and down, then back up. She's still looking at me. Her eyes are such an amazing green. Then, at the same time, we both lean in for a quick kiss. Her lips feel thick and warm against mine. I've never kissed a girl on the lips before. I've only ever kissed Zac. His chin is usually scratchy, but Jade's skin is soft and smooth. I think I like Jade's kiss much better than Zac's. And I think I'd like to do more than kiss Jade....

"Jilda," says Jade. She doesn't continue speaking, just keeps looking into my eyes.

"Jade," I reply and then don't know what to say. I've never been tongue-tied with girls in the past. But with Jade I'm experiencing sensations I've never had before.

"You feel something for me, don't you?" asks Jade.

I don't know how to answer. Of course I feel something, but I don't know how to articulate it. And if I say something, it will be disloyal to Zac, who has been so good to me.

Then I decide what I have to do. I tell her about Zac.

She looks at me as I speak, and I feel she can see into my soul.

Finally she says, "Oh." Just that. "Oh."

She squeezes my hand before we head off in opposite directions to our respective cabins. I wonder what Jade thinks of me now. Maybe she thinks I've been encouraging her when I haven't. Or not that I've been aware of. I just like being with her. A lot. I feel so confused….

We've had a hard day, but it had felt so good working alongside Jade, helping others in need. I realize as I lie here trying to fall asleep, that we've been so busy today I never had a chance to tell Jade about the ring. It's still around my neck, but it falls below the neckline of my T-shirt, so it hasn't been obvious.

I wonder whether anyone will come to claim the ring. I hope nobody will try and sneak into our cabin during the other two shifts when I'm not here and take things. If they're legitimate, they'll come at the time suggested, which is when Sheryl and I will be here.

Guess what, surprise, surprise, nobody comes to our door to claim the ring. So now I'm pretty sure the jewelry is stolen. As to the Pill packet, I think that will always remain a mystery—maybe the woman has been hiding the fact she is on the Pill from someone and decided Rosa's bag would be a good place to hide both that and the ring. I decide I need to take the ring to lost property, but of course there's no one looking after such a thing, as all the staff are occupied with more essential jobs like feeding passengers and cleaning up vomit. Maybe I should take it to the captain. But what could he do about it anyway? He'll be too busy keeping us on our course to mystery land. But I know I have to do something—it isn't mine and I can't keep it. No such thing as "finders keepers," really.

I finally fall asleep and dream of Jade. She's wearing the ring and smiling into my eyes.

CHAPTER TWELVE
DAY ELEVEN SHIP

AFTER I wheel Sheryl to breakfast, Jade and I meet up as arranged yesterday, and go down again to help the nurse out. I've taken some much-needed anti-nausea tablets, so my stomach is quite solid again. But the atmosphere between Jade and I has changed—I can sense a distance between us that wasn't there before I told her about Zac. She avoids looking directly into my eyes. I hope being busy together again today will close that gap and we can get on like before.

Or have I blown it by telling her about Zac?

The infirmary is overflowing with patients, and some are even lying down on the floor outside, as they can't get in. The medical center has now completely run out of supplies, so we can't do much except hold back people's hair as they puke, and rush around with paper or plastic bags toward anyone who starts heaving. The diarrhea is harder to deal with. Luckily there's plenty of water available, but I wonder how long the desalination pumps can keep up with the huge amount of water required.

I spend quite a lot of time with a woman who introduces herself as Lillian. Her three young children are so unwell, and she is just as ill, so she can't look after them properly by herself. She smiles weakly at me as I tend to her children while she lies on the floor, hair wet with sweat and exhausted.

Her children, Kite, Celine and Jon, are cute little things, and I feel sorry for them all as I wipe their brows and help them sip some water.

Even in such strange circumstances, I'm trying to enjoy being near Jade and getting to know her better. She seems very competent. She's so patient with people, cheering them up considerably with her friendliness, funny little jokes, and brilliant smile. As the day wears on, though, I feel more and more disheartened. I haven't managed to recover that close feeling with her.

About four o'clock in the afternoon, after Lillian and her children seem to have gotten over the worst of it, I suggest to Jade we wander upstairs to get some fresh air on the deck and have a break from our duties in the medical center. She encourages me to go by myself, and I'm disappointed, as I feel our closeness has evaporated. I don't want to beg, so I leave on my own.

I soon sense there's another mood developing on the ship. It isn't just all the passengers who are leaning over the edge of the railing looking green and gazing fixedly at the horizon, hoping for stomachs to settle. People are muttering in groups, and looking over shoulders to hear who's listening in.

I try to circumnavigate the ship to complete a full circuit of the promenade deck to stretch my legs and get some much-needed exercise, but it's hard going with the hordes of people. I find myself right at the front of the ship and manage to push into a spot on the railing as I drink in the invigorating, salty sea air. Looking ahead, I just wish I knew where we're going and what's eventually going to happen. I've been so busy helping with all the sick people, and now concerned my relationship with Jade is cooling, I haven't had much time to think about the bigger picture. But it really sinks in to me then, looking ahead at the rough, gray, empty seas.

Where are we?

It certainly isn't tropical waters and weather we're in anymore. *Have we traveled a lot farther south?* We can't have gone north toward the equator, as that would mean hot sun and steamy weather. We might have a storm in a tropical latitude, but it wouldn't be like this.

Maybe we're much farther south. But why would that be? What is down there apart from New Zealand—are we heading there? None of the passengers we've picked up know either. They keep telling us the same thing over and over – that they were told they wouldn't know where they're going until they arrive, as the organizers want it to be kept a secret. They want the country we're heading toward to be kept in the dark until we land, as otherwise we'll most probably be turned away.

Why has no one found us? I thought planes would be flying overhead and helicopters circling us. Or navy ships following us. It's so strange nobody has sighted us, but maybe that's the secrecy at work—the secrecy really has been successful. I suppose the ocean is vast, but I still thought modern technology could have helped find us by now. But seeing as our Wi-Fi hasn't worked from the time the ship was taken from Fiji, apparently we're in a blackout, giving and receiving no signals. And it's been several days since we last saw the other ships that were nearby when we first left Levy Archipelago—they've probably split up as far apart as possible so we would appear as separate ships, not a fleet.

But my musings are interrupted when Gavin and another of the original passengers, Mat, nudge their way in next to me. We get to talking about the situation and decide we've finally had enough of not knowing where we're going. It's driving us nuts. We can sort of understand the secrecy to ensure there was no security breach before the ships collected the other passengers, but what does it matter now if everyone knows, as there doesn't seem any way for us to get word out.

"What about my suggestion?" I ask.

Gavin fills Mat in on our previous discussion.

"I'm in," says Mat.

"Me too," I say.

"All right," says Gavin reluctantly.

So we hatch our plan. The men will pretend they're going to throw me overboard unless the captain divulges our destination. I have to act terrified. I'm secretly hoping that he'll quickly cave in and tell us, and that Jade will be so impressed with me being involved that she'll want to be close to me again.

We make our way up several metal stairways, until we reach the bridge. Gavin holds on to one of my arms and calls out in a loud voice that we want to speak to the captain.

"We aren't leaving until you come out and see us," he adds.

We make such a noise that the captain eventually emerges, bleary-eyed. I haven't seen him since the day of the baby's funeral, and he looks even worse for wear.

"Tell us where we're going, or we'll throw this girl overboard!" yells Gavin, just behind my ear.

"Calm down, calm down," says the captain. "This will not help anybody."

"But you of all people would know where we're heading. You're the captain!" says Mat, holding on to my other arm.

With all the commotion, a crowd has gathered around us, listening in, becoming agitated.

"I'm scared, please tell them," I whisper, trying to sound convincing. "I don't want to be tossed overboard."

"I'm afraid my hands are tied. I've been told my family will suffer if I tell anyone where we're going. This is not my choice, you know. I was not in on this plan. I am a hostage myself."

"Too bad," cries Gavin. "We have to know where we're going. It'll drive us crazy if we don't."

"It's not long now and you will know, I promise you," says the captain, trying to placate us.

"Not long is too late!" says Mat. "She's going overboard."

"Look," says the captain. He takes a deep breath as he seems to be carefully considering what he's going to say next.

We wait expectantly for him to continue.

"Okay. I'll be completely honest with you. The reason I can't tell you our destination is if we have to use our communication system for any reason, or are intercepted, someone may take advantage of the situation and our cover will be completely blown. That is why nobody can know where we're heading."

The captain turns to go back inside.

Gavin, Mat, and I just stand there, not sure what to do now.

"This girl really will be thrown overboard!" a deep voice booms from behind me.

I realize it's not Gavin or Mat saying this now. Someone else has taken up the call and the situation is suddenly getting totally out of hand.

Sinewy hands grab me, and I gasp. I'm wrenched out of Gavin's and Mat's gentle hold, and I'm being pushed through the crowds. I try to look around to see who has me in their grasp, but it's all happening so quickly and people are shoving in close, so I can only get brief glimpses of several men I don't recognize, with glaring eyes and messy hair.

I can't believe this is happening, how we lost control so quickly. I'm dragged down the flights of stairs, my feet tripping beneath me, and we're heading toward the deck railing. Gavin and Mat are trying to reach me but are being forcibly held back by several burly men. I'm now genuinely frightened.

The crowds are parting—it seems nobody is willing or able to help me. I so wish Jade was with me. These people are finally desperate and want answers, and I'm apparently the way they're going to try and get some. I'm being lifted up, my feet no longer touching the deck.

Oh God, how has it come to this?

Strong hands hold me high, and I can feel myself teetering over the edge of the metal rail. The wind whips my hair around and flicks it into my eyes. Am I really going to end up in the icy-looking water far below, or are they bluffing?

I hear a cry. "Stop! Stop! Let her down!" It's the captain, who has followed us and is right behind the men. "Think about what you're doing. She is a human being who has done no harm."

"*Tell us where we are going*," yells one of my captors, "*and we will let her go!*"

A chant begins, with others on the deck joining in.

"Where are we going? Where are we going?"

Some people start to clap and stomp their feet in rhythm with the words, and soon the noise is deafening.

"*Where are we going? Where are we going?*"

The captain finally understands they really mean business. I feel myself being lifted higher, my toes now barely touching the top of the railing. The men are holding me by my calves and wrists, and it's all I can do to try and keep my balance I'm swaying so much. Suddenly I'm pushed, but my fall is broken as rough hands keep gripping my ankles. My face thumps into the side of the ship below the railing, and I can feel blood pour hot from my nose. I'm hanging upside down, outside the railing, and I'm screaming and bawling at the same time, stomach rolling. My fists beat against the metallic hull of the ship.

"*All right!*" I hear the captain yell. "Bring her back up and I'll tell you."

I'm yanked back up, and I grip each railing as I come up to help keep myself steady. I slide over the top railing and slump backward onto the deck. Blood and tears pour down my face, and I'm heaving, but I manage not to vomit. I don't care who sees. I'm just so glad I'm fully back on board, with the wooden deck firmly underneath my back. I don't feel I'll be able to stand up for a while anyway, my legs are shaking so much.

"Well?" shouts one of the men.

"Australia. We're headed to Australia," concedes the captain, palms outstretched.

"Australia? Australia?"

"Yes, Australia. Satisfied?"

There's muttering that gets louder. There's excitement, I can tell. I can't believe nobody asks exactly where in Australia. They are content to hear the magic word *Australia*.

Gavin and Mat are released and make their way toward me. They say they're so sorry for what's happened. It wasn't meant to turn out that way.

One of the women in the crowd kindly proffers a tissue to wipe my tears. But when she leans down close to me, she suddenly stands straight upright again, pointing an accusing finger at me.

She yells out loudly: "That's mine! You thief!"

I look down at my chest. The ring on its chain has tipped out from under my neckline, from when I was hanging upside down over the ship's rail. It's dangling there with Rosa's shell charm against the front of my T-shirt for everyone to see.

"Where did you get it?" she continues shouting at me. "That's my family heirloom!"

She leans over toward me again and tries to snatch the chain from my neck. I can smell her flowery perfume she's so close. After several yanks it gives way, the chain breaking against the back of my neck. The shell charm slides off one end of the chain, and I grab it up. Rosa will kill me if I lose that, and she won't be too happy about the broken chain either.

The woman triumphantly brandishes the broken chain with the ring hanging from it in front of my face, swinging it to and fro. I rub my neck where the chain had snapped against it. The whole area stings.

The captain comes over to see what all the fuss is about.

"What's happening here now?" he asks, trying to calm the situation.

Still rubbing my neck, I try to explain how I found the ring—but it's difficult being heard due to the accusations being hurled at me, not only by the woman but others around her in the crowd who are taking her side.

By now a man who seems to be her husband is standing beside her and listening carefully to my story. He tries to calm his wife down, saying, "Maybe what she says is true."

The woman looks at her husband enquiringly, still angry. She stops swinging the chain.

The husband continues. "The ring was not stolen on this ship. It was originally stolen on Levy Archipelago, and the thief must have brought it on board, pretending it to be one of their precious possessions, and stashed it in a bag belonging to this girl's family."

His wife hasn't given up yet. "But she had my ring—she's a thief!"

"Give her a break," says Gavin.

"This girl isn't from Levy Archipelago—she's never even set foot on the island, so how could she have stolen it from you there?" her husband asks.

I look at the husband, hanging on to his every word, as he seems to believe me.

"My wife was frantically looking for it everywhere when we were told to pack our things," he continues.

The woman's face changes as the facts sink in. "It's true. I was racking my brains trying to remember when the last time was I had seen this ring, and it had been months, I realized. I gave up looking for it when it was time to leave the house to board the ship. I was heartbroken I had to leave without it, as it belonged to my grandmother and I really wanted it with me in our new lives."

She jams the ring onto her finger. She holds her hand with arm outstretched, admiring her ring and smiling.

She then turns back to me and says, "Tell me exactly who had it in their possession, then."

"Knowing that won't help matters," says the captain. "I'm glad the ring seems to have found its rightful owner, so let's leave it at that. It's just a reminder that you all must be careful of your possessions on board."

The woman opens her mouth as if to continue, but her husband says to let it rest. She finally gives me the chain back, apologizing for having snapped it. I'm furious she's broken it, but I just want the whole incident to be over. I slip the chain into my pocket along with Rosa's charm.

I look up to see Jade's pale determined face as she pushes her way through the crowd.

She must have come to find me!

Jade finally reaches me. She helps me into a sitting position and the others draw away to create some space. Jade gently wipes my tears with a tissue while another woman helps stem my nosebleed with the corner of her skirt. I try not to think of the germs on the skirt—I'm just so grateful it all seems to be over. Suddenly somebody starts to clap, and then the clapping is taken up by another, then another. This is friendly applause, not the ominous sound of just moments before. Soon everybody is applauding and smiling at me and saying, "Thank you, thank you," as if it's me taking them to Australia. They must think of Australia as the land of milk and honey.

All I want to do is go to my cabin, but it's hours until my shift starts again. Through the fog of my emotions, a hand slips into mine and helps me onto my feet—Jade. Now I feel utterly rescued. The distance between us disappears in that instant.

CHAPTER THIRTEEN
DAY TWELVE SHIP

THIS MORNING we're awoken at seven by an announcement to make our final pack up before we leave the cabins at 8:00 a.m., and to place our cases outside our doors so we won't have to go into the cabins again. We are to leave the towels on the bathroom floor under the vanity unit so the next shift won't trip over them, and to put all our sheets into the pillowcases and put them into the wardrobe. Only one more shift is going to use the cabin today. So we must be arriving in port before the third shift has their turn. Sheryl then gets into a panic about her sister's bags, and we set off to her old cabin to retrieve them. In all the fuss of people packing up, no one is bothered that we take Sheryl's sister's luggage—if anything they're relieved not to have to deal with it. We put her bags outside our cabin with all the rest. It's a huge mound now.

It's hard to fill in the day, we're so restless, knowing that finally something is going to happen. Will we be on land at last after so many days at sea? And where will that be? The captain had said Australia, but with Australia's long coastline it really could be just about anywhere. During the day we can see other ships in the distance, getting closer to us. They aren't navy ships—they must be some of the others we'd last seen when we were leaving Levy Archipelago all those days ago.

Finally a hump of land appears and we sail closer and closer to it.

Land! I hadn't realized I missed it so much. Life at sea has almost become normal after so long. I wish we had some binoculars to have a good look at where we are arriving. Mum had taken ours with her on that day excursion in Fiji, which seems like a lifetime ago now so much has happened since then.

As our ship steams closer to land, Jade and I manage to get a vantage point from one of the top decks. Our ship is in the lead, and as we look back over our shoulders, we can see the other massive ships are moving in closer, sailing in an arrow shape, with us at its tip. Three ships sail diagonally on either side, the third ones the most distant, and directly behind us in a straight line are three more ships, one behind the other. It's an incredible spectacle.

"There *are* ten!" shouts Jade. "They've actually gone and done it."

We can see the decks of the other ships are crowded with passengers, all gazing toward the ever-nearing land.

As Jade and I gaze into the distance, a strange sensation comes over me.

"I know where we are," I cry in wonder. Tears start rolling down my cheeks.

"Where?"

"We're coming into Hobart!"

"How do you know?"

It must all just look like a hazy bundle of cliffs in the distance to her.

"The land. I know the shape of the land so well, from when Dad takes us sailing!"

"Wow!" She hugs me tight.

"The Iron Pot. We've just come round the Iron Pot!"

"Iron Pot?"

"Yes, see that rocky little island with the lighthouse on it?" I point to the familiar landmark.

As we sail up the River Derwent, I can see kunanyi/Mount Wellington towering over the city. Looking back, we can see behind us some of the other ships peeling away. They're heading to Blackmans Bay and Kingston beach. Yet others sail off in the direction of Howrah and Bellerive beaches.

The four ships, one behind the other, that made the arrow shaft shape keep steaming up the river toward the harbor.

Our ship and three others are sailing right into the main Hobart docks, while the others must be going to beach themselves on the sand. There are no docks where they're heading.

As we get closer, I can make out individual trees, houses, cars, and then people, and even dogs. Hundreds of people are lining the shore watching us coming in. Helicopters are now circling above, cameras pointing down at us. We wave enthusiastically up at them.

When we come into port, the authorities try to stop us by putting police boats between the ships and the shore. But it soon becomes clear the ships are stopping for no one, and that if the police in their small boats persist their lives will be in danger.

Finally we come right into the Hobart docks and pull up at the pier. I know Hobart can take four giant cruise ships in one go, as that has happened regularly in the past in peak tourist season, when the megaliths fill everyone's view. Hobart being on hilly slopes, most houses have a direct view of the river, and the cruise ships always look massive against the low skyline of Hobart. The only thing that dwarfs the ships is the eternal shape of kunanyi/Mount Wellington, our mother mountain who watches over us. But she's never witnessed anything like this. Nothing this weird has happened since the day Europeans sailed into the harbor for the first time and changed Tasmania forever.

"Order, order," cry the crew members, trying to avoid panic. They are vastly outnumbered.

We want to get off, and fast, but we know any panic could trigger a stampede, and with the number of passengers on board, people could be trampled. Injuries or even death could occur if things got out of hand. So we wait patiently until we are given the go-ahead to disembark. I sit on my suitcase and have my hand luggage plus Mum's and Rosa's luggage on either side of me. Jade has gone off to get her parents' bags, and I'm minding hers as well. Sheryl sits there in her wheelchair surrounded by luggage too. Jade finally staggers back through the crowds, dragging two more cases with hand luggage balanced on top. How on earth are we going to get this colossal amount of luggage off the ship? Eight suitcases and eight pieces of hand luggage!

"I walked on to this ship, and I'm walking off," says Sheryl. "Let's stack the suitcases up in my wheelchair."

I look down at Sheryl's swollen feet and try to protest, but she's determined.

"It's the only way," she says.

She's right. We put the biggest case on the bottom and then place them in diminishing size until the smallest suitcase is on the top. We still have eight pieces of hand luggage to deal with. One stacked on top of another makes four piles.

I say, "I'll push the wheelchair and steady the stack of suitcases, and you two will have to drag two pieces of hand luggage in each hand."

We look at each other, then burst out laughing. It's totally ridiculous. But doable.

Our gangway is lowered and passengers pour off the ship, dragging or carrying their luggage. It's a human tsunami, and even though there are hundreds of police and people dressed in army uniforms on the wharf, the authorities can't stop the wave of humanity. I can't see Marta or Simone anywhere among the crowds to say goodbye.

Jade, Sheryl, and I finally get off the boat. It's really hard with the wheelchair covered in cases so high I can't see over the top of them. I have to tip the wheelchair back a bit on its wheels so the suitcases will stay more or less horizontal as we slowly make our way down the gangplank. Sheryl's and Jade's piles of hand luggage keep tipping over and they have to continually bend down and pick them up again, rebalancing one on top of the other.

It's so difficult juggling all the luggage, and I know we won't get very far like this. Suddenly I have an idea. Leaving all the bags with Jade and Sheryl, I rush over to Mures, the seafood restaurant on the docks, where Mum is good friends with the manager, Sally. She hugs me until she almost squeezes me half to death—she knows all about how my ship was hijacked and then disappeared. She wants to ring Mum straightaway to let her know I'm safe, but I say I want to surprise her, just turning up unannounced at our front door. Sally finally agrees, and also says she's happy to store our bags for us in a room off the restaurant's kitchen until Mum comes to collect them. I want to keep Sheryl's and Jade's bags with us, though, as that is all they have with them in the world at the moment, whereas I have other stuff at home I can wear and use until the bags are all collected.

With Jade pushing Sheryl, who has her and Jade's hand luggage across her lap now, handbag balanced on top of that, I trundle Jade's and Sheryl's suitcases up the footpath to the Franklin Square bus stop. No authorities stand in our way. There are just too many people milling around the docks to deal with everyone coming off the ships.

We catch the bus to Blackmans Bay. It's so strange being in such a familiar environment after everything that's happened. As the bus rounds the corner, we can see two of the massive ships on the sand. The beach is swarming with people. We hop off, and everyone else in the bus, including the bus driver, gets off too. They want to go down and see the action for themselves. I'm pushing Sheryl now, and Jade's dragging the bags up D'Entrecasteaux Street. When I see my house at the end of the cul-de-sac, tears sting my eyes. Home.

But nobody is home. Of course, Mum and Rosa will be down at the beach to see what's happening. People in the street are streaming down to the seaside to see the giant cruise ships parked on the beach.

I grab the two pieces of hand luggage off Sheryl's lap, and leave their luggage in the porch, as I don't have a key with me. We head down to the shore. It's easier pushing Sheryl then, as we're now going downhill, but I have to be careful the wheelchair doesn't run away from me with gravity. The last thing we need now is for an accident to happen to Sheryl.

Those with houses on the esplanade or at the hotel and the pizza restaurant have a bird's-eye view without needing to leave their comfortable seats, and watch on, drinks in hand. You'd think they were witnessing a festival from a comfortable distance.

CHAPTER FOURTEEN
DAY ONE SHORE

IT TAKES about half an hour for me to find Mum and Rosa. They see me and push their way through the crowds. Mum clutches me so hard I feel like I'm going to break in two. Rosa grabs me too, and we hug so tight. She tugs the hem of my dress, as she recognizes it as one of hers. We're so overwhelmed we can't speak. No words can describe our sensations and feelings. None.

Jade and Sheryl stare from me to Rosa and back again. They're speechless as well.

We forget in the heat of the moment that we're so alike, and that it stuns others the first time they see us together.

I pull out Dad's gift for Rosa, which I'd put in my pocket when I realized we were heading into Hobart. Rosa opens the package and immediately pops the earrings into her ears. Then she and I simultaneously reach out and pull an earring gently from each other's ear and place it in our own earlobe. We now have our own matching earrings, and not a word has been spoken. I have the turtles, and Rosa has the seahorses. I decide to tell her all about her broken chain later. I don't want to spoil the homecoming mood.

Mum immediately rings Dad. He's witnessing the same spectacle from the opposite side of the river, on the Eastern Shore. He says he saw three ships heading over to his side of the river, with one of the ships coming onto Bellerive Beach. The other two he can see in the distance are on Howrah Beach. Bellerive Beach is swarming with thousands upon thousands of people too. As he is speaking to Mum, I'm trying to grab the phone off her so I can speak to him. I'm so happy to hear his voice again. He's excited, and I can hear the warmth in his voice as well as sheer relief. But it's difficult to make out what he's saying over the noise of the crowds on the beach. And there's background noise on his end too.

"Honey," he says, "I'm afraid I've got to go. We've decided to open up the Blundstone Arena, so at least some of these people can sit in a proper seat, rather than just sitting in the sand. And we've got to give them access to toilets, pronto. The few cubicles here on the beach are nowhere near enough."

I hadn't thought about toilets for all these people coming off the ship. But I realize now, you can't just suddenly find enough toilets for an extra third of the number of people who live in the whole of Hobart.

I know the arena can seat nineteen thousand or so people, and then there is the central oval that's covered in grass they can sit on too. But that will soon be completely packed with the thirty-six thousand or so people who would have disembarked from three overcrowded ships on Howrah and Bellerive Beaches. How on earth are all these people going to be dealt with?

There is nothing much Mum, Rosa, Jade, Sheryl, and I can do on Blackmans Bay beach, and so we decide it's better to go home, to at least reduce the huge numbers by five. Not that five will really make any difference among the sea of humanity. But it's overwhelming and anyway, we all need a rest after such drama. Or even collapse.

As we walk up the street, I see Zac sitting on our porch looking at his phone. He looks up when he hears us coming and runs down the street, lifting me in his arms and kissing me all over my face. He's laughing and looks so happy, and all I feel is guilt as I stiffen in his arms. This just doesn't seem right anymore. He puts me down again, a puzzled look on his face.

We put the television on as soon as we get inside, and all the stations are filled with the story, as regular programs are interrupted to update the situation. Apparently the prime minister is flying down to take control, and the army is being called in. I sit down next to Jade on the couch, and Zac sits next to me on my other side. I squirm with discomfort. I'm so glad the television is taking up all of our attention, as I can't look Zac in the eye. Zac grabs my hand and starts stroking his thumb across the back of it while still looking at the TV. His hand feels big and clammy and possessive, and his thumb skin is rough. I hold it for a little while, then gently slip my hand out of his grasp and put both my hands together in my lap. In my peripheral vision I can see him glance at me, but I don't turn to face him.

Later, when the prime minister arrives, we see her being interviewed. She says the army chief, General Stockard, will be in control, and all citizens must follow the general's orders. Frances Stockard is a person who inspires confidence.

Buses have come streaming into Hobart from all over Tasmania to deal with the large numbers of people. Some people are already in the Blundstone Arena, while others are bussed to the Convention Centre, Princes Wharves 1 and 2, the IMAS building, the Brooke Street Pier, some of the large buildings in the Macquarie Port area, to the Showgrounds, the Derwent Entertainment Centre, and to all the local school auditoriums. This gives immediate shelter or at least somewhere to sit, and access to running water. It's so pathetic to see the citizens of Levy Archipelago clutching their possessions or dragging suitcases with wheels so sand clogged they won't turn properly. Their possessions must indeed seem so precious, as that is the culmination of all their previous lives—the most important things they'd decided they just had to save from the rising waters.

In the television interview, General Stockard says, "First of all, there are approximately one hundred and twenty thousand people who require shelter and food and access to bathrooms. Basically, that is a third again of the current population of Hobart. Every large building in the immediate and greater Hobart area will initially be used for shelter while we sort everyone out."

The uniformed man standing behind her nods his head to show agreement. People being interviewed always seem to have "nodders" behind them these days.

General Stockard continues, "We will have to close the schools for the time being. Once we have processed the numbers and identified the family groups, every resort, hotel, motel, inn, guesthouse, bed-and-breakfast, campground, public space, theater, and school in Tasmania will have to open their doors to those seeking shelter. We will be providing mattresses and bedding in all the large wharf buildings too. We ask any person who is willing to take people into their homes once the paperwork is finalized to contact us, as that will help the situation enormously."

Mum, Rosa, and I all exchange glances at this. We already have a full house now with Sheryl and Jade, but we know they probably won't be staying long. I feel so sad knowing Jade will be leaving me soon. After they do leave, maybe we can help out some others from Levy Archipelago. I haven't had a chance to tell Mum and Rosa much about Marta and Jonas yet, but I'm sure they'll be agreeable for them to come and stay with us for a while, once the others have gone back to their respective homes. Not that I want Jade to go anywhere. I wish she could stay with us here forever, or at least in Hobart so I can be near her.

The general says, "These people are environmental refugees who come in peace from Levy Archipelago. I have spoken to their leader, and he says all they want is to be together in one country, not split up and sent to different countries as they had been offered previously. These people cannot be sent home, as there is virtually no home to go to after the last devastating tsunami that swept across their islands."

Behind the general, we can see hundreds of protesters holding up placards and shouting into megaphones similar sayings to what are written on their signs: "Send them back!" and "Not welcome here!" and "Go back to where you came from!" and "They'll take our jobs!" Some of them are waving Australian flags, and others are shouting, "Aussie, Aussie, Aussie. Oi! Oi! Oi!" It's the first time I feel ashamed of being an Australian, seeing the lack of welcome these poor people like Marta and Jonas are receiving.

The general is doing her best to speak over their ruckus. Although she's interrupted constantly, she continues, determined to get her message across.

"We must show compassion to these people who have lost their homes due to no fault of their own—only through the force of history that led them to live in such a vulnerable area of the world. The world and all its greed has caused the climate change that has led to the situation we find ourselves in today. We need Tasmanians' help and cooperation. Your cooperation."

We hang on to every word of her long speech.

The protesters near the general don't let up, though. They just get increasingly agitated the more she speaks.

Mum looks at Jade and Sheryl.

Mum says, "Well, you two are staying here with us anyway, no matter what else the general says, until everything is sorted for you to go back home. You are welcome to stay as long as you have to, or as long as you like."

"Thank you so much," says Sheryl. "But hopefully it won't take too long to get a flight back to Sydney. I just want to be with my husband. And see my sister."

"Thanks," says Jade. "I'd love that." She smiles straight at me.

Zac looks at her, then back at me.

"I think I'll go home," he says.

He stands up and looks down at me. Any other time in the past I would see him out, so we could have a private goodbye away from prying eyes. But it just seems wrong today.

"Aren't you walking me out, Jilda?" he says, sounding hurt.

I stand up. I owe it to him to talk to him on his own. He has such a wounded expression on his face, and he's been my boyfriend for almost six months now.

When we get outside, straightaway he says, "What's with you and the leso?"

I'm so glad he called her that, as it makes it so much easier to say what I'm about to say.

"I don't think we should be together anymore, Zac."

"Why not? Because of her?"

"Well… I don't know… maybe…."

"You're kidding. You'd rather be with her than me? I don't believe it."

"I don't know what I'm feeling at the moment, Zac. I've just had a really strange experience—"

"Looks like it!"

"I need some space, Zac. To work things out." I can hear my voice quavering, but I'm trying to be brave.

"Don't worry, I'll give you some space. Plenty of it."

He turns on his heels and stomps off. But after only a few steps he comes to an abrupt halt and turns around. His arms are outstretched, palms turned outward, facing me.

"I really missed you, you know, Jilda. I've been so worried about you."

"I know."

"And what about your party? It's supposed to be at my parents' place next Saturday!"

"I know. We'll have to call the party off. People will just think it's because of what's been happening to me."

"Except they won't know the real reason, will they? You've got the hots for Jade…."

Zac turns around again and storms off up the street. I feel an ache in my heart. We'd been pretty good together, or so I'd thought, until I met Jade and my whole world changed.

When I go back inside, Jade looks at me, then looks away. I sit down again and pretend I'm still interested in the television. I wish I could hold her hand, but I don't think the others would be ready to see us like that yet.

THE REST of the afternoon Mum, Rosa, and I tell each other what happened since we were last together. Mum wants me to go first, and she and Rosa keep interrupting asking more questions. I'm exhausted with the telling and Jade pitches in to help explain details, but she's really good at getting cues from me about what to leave out. Then Mum and Rosa tell us everything that happened to them. How they'd felt when they arrived at the pier after their excursion and found the ship gone. About the swarms of angry passengers stranded on the dock. How they'd stayed with a local couple in a colorful house on a hill, the daily queues in the boiling sun at the waterfront while trying to get details of what was happening, having to buy clothes from the market as they only had what they stood up in, and their enforced flight home. They tell me about all the emails, meetings, and phone calls Mum, Dad, and Rosa had with the ship's company, politicians, and journalists to get some answers and action. Apparently Rosa had organized petitions and protests in front of Parliament House. What a sister she is. Then Mum and Rosa describe their surreal witnessing of the ten huge cruise ships surging up the River Derwent, two of them filling their view from our lounge-room window when they rammed onto the beach. It was strange hearing it all from their point of view. As we speak I can see the worry lines slowly fade from Mum's face, and she starts looking like her normal self again.

Much later this afternoon, Mum and I go to collect the luggage from Mures, and Sally treats us to a huge pile of fish and chips to take home to save us cooking dinner. Dad finally manages to free himself, and races over to our house to see me. He gives me the best hug he's ever given me in my life, and I can feel his heart pounding in his chest as he holds me tight. He seems reluctant to ever let me go. He finally releases me, ruffling my hair.

"My baby," he says, his voice so full of love and relief.

Luckily there are stacks of fish and chips, so he doesn't have to miss out. He stuffs a few chips in his mouth, but I can tell he's not really interested in eating. He just wants to hear everything I've got to say. He can't take his eyes off me. Poor Dad had wanted to fly to Fiji to help, but Mum had insisted he stay behind in case I tried to contact him or even turned up before she and Rosa got home. Apparently it had taken several days for the authorities to organize their return to Australia from Fiji with no passports or proper paperwork.

This evening after we've finished eating, we have to sort out sleeping arrangements and Dad leaves to go back to his place. I can see he doesn't want to go, and I feel sorry for him.

Jade is to sleep on the foldout sofa in the lounge room, and I give Sheryl my room and hop in with Rosa. It's so nice to snuggle up in the same bed as Rosa after missing her so much. Sheryl says she doesn't like to put us out, but I assure her she isn't—she's actually doing us a favor, as it will give Rosa and me a chance to catch up.

"What's with you and Jade?" asks Rosa as soon as we're alone in her room later that night.

"What do you mean?" I ask, stalling for time, hoping she'll say it first.

"Come on, Jilda, it's obvious something's going on between you two."

"I really, really like her," I say. "Do you think she likes me?"

"I'm sure she does. Haven't you seen the way she looks at you? I wish Andy would look that way at me."

"How does she look at me?"

"Her eyes follow you everywhere. And she sort of smiles all the time whenever she looks in your direction," says Rosa.

"Does she? I'm stoked. I think she's really cool."

"What about Zac? You never took any interest in girls before."

"I told him this afternoon that I don't think we should go out anymore."

"Wow! What did he say?"

"He called her a leso...."

"That's not nice."

"I suppose he's hurt I prefer Jade to him. And probably can't understand it either."

"Oh no. That means we can't have our party at his house!"

"I'm so sorry, Rosa."

"I'm sorry too. That sounded so selfish of me. I don't care about the party. I'm just so glad you're safely home again. I don't think anyone really thought the party was going to happen anyway, because of all the uncertainty. Nothing's been organized."

"Thank God for that."

"Jade does seem nice. Lucky thing. What's going to happen to you two now?"

"I don't know. I wish I knew. She'll be going back home to the US pretty soon, I suppose. As soon as her parents organize her flights. I wish I could go with her."

"Sorry, Jilda, it's more like back to school for you. And me. Or at least, when it reopens, though it may take a while to find alternative accommodation for all the people staying there."

"You haven't been back to school yet?"

"No, Mum understands. It was only a couple of days anyway. I just couldn't concentrate with you away. And we were too busy organizing the protest and things."

"It'll be great not having to go to school—I'll be able to spend more time with Jade until she goes back."

"I don't think too many other schoolkids will be complaining either!"

"I can't believe I'm home again. It all seems so weird."

Rosa squeezes my hand.

"Tell me more about what happened," she asks.

So we lie there in the dark as I fill her in on all the gory details. I left a few things out when talking to Mum and her earlier, like the time I was nearly thrown off the ship, as

I thought Mum would freak. I just have to unload to Rosa, though. I'm so used to never keeping anything from her. Rosa grips my hand tighter and says, "Oh my God" over and over again.

"There's one more detail I have to tell you about that time they tried to toss me from the ship."

"Yes?" asks Rosa warily.

I tell her about what happened to her chain, and she assures me she isn't upset at all.

"It's only a chain, Jilda. A broken chain is nothing compared to how broken our lives would've been if you hadn't come home safely."

My tale finally comes to an end, and we drift off to sleep.

During the night I wake up thirsty, so I carefully get out of bed, trying not to disturb Rosa, and creep to the kitchen to have a glass of water. I have to pass Jade sleeping on the sofa bed and stop to look at her. A shaft of moonlight lies across her face and I can clearly make out her features. She really is beautiful. Her dark hair fans across the pillow and her skin is smooth. She looks so peaceful lying there, but when I pass her again after having my drink, she begins to stir. Her arms and legs are moving, and she starts to thrash around and groan a little. Her dreams must have suddenly turned into nightmares. I don't know whether to wake her from whatever is disturbing her, but just as quickly she calms down again, so I decide to let her be. But I can't resist stroking her hair away from her forehead and pressing the lightest of kisses there. Suddenly I feel her hand in my hair and she pulls me toward her. Mouths, skin, hair all meld into one and I slide into bed beside her. She is warm and soft and I stay there, our legs entwined, until the dawn is breaking.

I slip out of her bed and creep back to Rosa's bedroom so Sheryl and Mum won't find us there together. I don't think Mum will mind too much, although I know she'll be surprised—all right, shocked—about my feelings for Jade, but Sheryl might have a heart attack, and I don't want to cause that after all she's been through.

Back in Rosa's bed, I think about Jade and how lucky I am to have met her. The circumstances of our meeting were horrendous, but I'm sure we'll never forget each other, no matter what happens, because we've become close so quickly due to our strange shared experiences. If we hadn't been hijacked, we may have passed the entire cruise without ever noticing each other among the throngs of passengers on the ship. Surely I'm not feeling thankful for the hijacking, but in a way I am, because it meant Jade and I crossed paths and got to know each other. And I've found out more about myself than I ever realized. Discovered myself. Who I really am.

CHAPTER FIFTEEN
FOLLOWING DAYS SHORE

SHERYL MANAGES to get a flight back home to Sydney this morning. Jade has been busy discussing flight options with her parents, but nothing has been confirmed yet. I think Jade is stalling about returning home. I hope she is anyway. She's on her gap year, or whatever they call it in the US, after finishing high school, so there's no real rush for her to leave.

I feel quite sad knowing I'll be saying goodbye to Sheryl today, as she and I have become real supports for each other and she's almost like another grandmother to me. I wonder whether I'll ever see her again. I won't let my brain go anywhere near thinking about Jade leaving.

At the airport we promise to catch up with Sheryl if ever we're in Sydney, and she says when, or even if, her husband is well enough to travel again, they might come to Tasmania for a holiday. She declares she has sworn off ever going overseas again. And certainly never on a cruise.

"So you won't ever go to... what's the name of that place you come from again, Jade?" I ask.

"Kissimmee," she says, putting the emphasis on the first syllable with a twinkle in her eye.

So I do. Right on the lips.

Sheryl gasps and glances away, Mum looks surprised, but Rosa smiles widely. Jade's face is flushed, but she seems really pleased. I want everyone to know how I feel about Jade.

After we've said farewell to Sheryl, we show Jade round the local sights so she can get to know Hobart a little. We scour the Salamanca Markets for some typical Tasmanian souvenirs like wood products and socks made to look like Tassie devils for Jade to take home to her parents one day, and eat hot, salty scallops from one of the seafood punts at Constitution Dock, feeding each other fat, vinegary, hand-cut chips.

The four ships are still at the docks, and tourists and locals alike are flocking to see them and take photos. The air is abuzz with excitement and speculation. We go up close to "our" ship, and I get goose bumps looking at it. The decks are now empty of people, and already it's hard to imagine the thousands on board, the crowding and the hot-bedding. And the fear and uncertainty.

After that we take selfies on the rocks at the summit of kunanyi/Mount Wellington, where on this bright, clear afternoon we can see forever. I point out all the local landmarks to Jade. From our vantage point up so high, the ten ships, all still in the same positions from when we first arrived, look spectacular. The River Derwent looks like a giant movie set.

"I wonder when they'll remove the ships," says Rosa.

"I'm not sure what's going on," says Mum. "I suppose they'll sail them away when they know where they all originate from."

We heard on the news this morning that the passengers on our ship were the only ones who'd had to endure hot-bedding, as the other ships were decommissioned cruise ships, no longer in service, that had been emptied out and set up to hold a massive number of people with enough beds for all on board. So it seems it was the result of a carefully thought-out long-term plan to relatively comfortably evacuate the entire population of Levy Archipelago simultaneously. Something must have happened at the last minute, so that they suddenly needed our ship too. Our ship mustn't have been part of their original plan. The other ships would still have been crowded, but at least those passengers didn't have to deal with the annoying hot-bedding system and irregular hours. The authorities are still investigating how it all came about.

This evening after dinner, Rosa, Jade, and I sit drinking green tea on our veranda, looking out to the river and down onto the rammed ships on Blackmans Bay beach. Mum's gone out, catching up with friends she couldn't make time for when she was so busy worrying about me and campaigning for the authorities to find us.

"It seems such a waste," I say.

"What is?" asks Jade.

"Those nine emptied-out old ships."

"Yes…," says Rosa. She knows I get some strange ideas sometimes and is used to hearing me out.

"Well, one of them could be used to collect all the animals left behind."

"What?" says Rosa. You can tell I've really surprised her this time.

I tell Rosa and Jade about the conversations Sheryl and I had in our room with Marta and Simone, of how heartbroken the locals are at having to leave their precious animals behind. How they were told there was only room for people on the ships, not their pets and livestock as well. I tell Rosa and Jade I've already had nightmares about thousands of animals wild-eyed and gasping, then drowning, being swallowed up by the sea.

"We just can't leave them to drown," I say. "It's wrong. Animals are just as important as people."

"You're so right," says Jade. "Let's do something about it."

"Like what?" says Rosa.

So we devise a plan. I remember the half-full tin of red paint in the storeroom, left over from when we painted the window frames and skirting boards in the kitchen. The drop sheet made from thick hemp-like material that we used for painting doesn't have too many paint splotches on it. We spread it out on the storeroom floor and paint in large red letters: "RESCUE THE ANIMALS!" and underneath that, "DON'T LET THEM DROWN!"

Luckily Mum won't be back for hours. We have to hope she doesn't need to go into the storeroom where we've got the drop sheet spread out on the floor drying. We don't want to tell her what we're up to. She'll try and stop us. I know it.

I set the alarm for 4:00 a.m. and stuff the clock under my pillow so it won't be too loud and wake Mum. Mum sleeps like a rock, anyway, but just in case.... We've agreed Rosa will stay behind, so that if Mum does wake up she can say Jade and I have gone for an early morning walk on the beach because of the beautiful full moon—we don't want her to freak out that we've disappeared so soon after I've returned. She might have a heart attack or a nervous breakdown, and she certainly doesn't deserve either of those after all she's been through.

I creep out and wake up Jade with a gentle kiss on her forehead. We roll up the drop sheet in the storeroom—the paint is mercifully dry, as we don't want our words to streak and be unreadable. I grab several lengths of rope Dad left behind when he moved out—thankfully sailors have lots of spare rope.

I roll the rope into coils and loop them up our arms and over our shoulders—we'll need four of them. I find two torches and give one to Jade. We each pick up one end of the drop sheet cylinder, as it is quite heavy, and slip out the door into the night. There is a full moon, so at least that part of the story Rosa might possibly have to tell Mum is true. As is the beach part. The most important part, of course, will come out later, after the deed has been done.

Jade and I soon reach the beach and are startled to see a security guard near one of the ships. We hadn't thought of that. We realize they would have to have some sort of security to stop unauthorized people clambering all over the ships. We stand behind some trees, prop our weighty cylinder against a tree trunk, and watch him for a while, uncertain what to do. He sits down on a wooden bench, looking at his phone, then gets up again and wanders off toward the toilet block. He looks over his shoulder before he enters the building, then goes in.

"It's now or never," I whisper to Jade and she nods.

We hoist up the sheet again and sprint across the sand as fast as we can, considering the bundles we're juggling. We go straight into the guts of the closer ship, through the huge makeshift hatch which had been dropped down onto the sand where the people had poured out. It's pitch-black in here, despite the full moon outside, and I'm so glad I thought of the torches. We climb up through the ship until we reach the deck above the life boats. We look down and there's no sign of the security guard. Let's hope he stays in the toilet for a while. He's got his phone, so that might keep him interested for a longer time than necessary.

We have to work out how to tie the drop sheet to the ship so that it hangs down on the side and won't flap around too much. It's easy enough to shape the corners of the drop sheet into a loopy knot and tie a rope to each one. We then spread out the length of the drop sheet and firmly tie two of the ropes to the ship's rail, leaving the bottom of the drop sheet swinging free. We now have to get down to where the lifeboats are and tie the bottom ropes on there. We race down the steps, one eye out for the guard, who thankfully still seems occupied in the toilets. We tie the lower ropes onto the davits and we're done and out of there, racing across the sand and up the hill. Safely back home, we go out onto the veranda to look down at our handiwork. The full moon is shining on the white drop sheet and our large words in red paint stand out clearly even from this distance. I take a photo it looks so good.

It's hard to go back to sleep after all that excitement, and it's almost dawn anyway. I get Jade and myself a glass of orange juice each, and we huddle closely together on the veranda in the cool morning air, sipping our drinks and whispering so as not to disturb the others.

When Rosa and Mum get up, Rosa races straight to the front windows.

"Awesome!" she says.

"It is, isn't it," I reply smugly.

Jade and I share a smile and a congratulatory knuckle tap.

"What's going on?" asks Mum.

No one answers, but she follows the direction of our eyes.

"Wow! Look at that!" Mum exclaims.

She looks back at us.

"Tell me you don't have anything to do with it," she says.

"No can do, Mum," I confess.

"There'll be trouble, I know it," she says.

"Who cares?" I say. "It'll be worth it. They'll really have to do something about the animals now that they know."

As I speak Jade says, "Oh no...."

Someone is taking down our sign already.

But that night we find out our handiwork was not in vain. Some early bird has taken a photo of our sign and sent it to the local news. There's a lot of speculation about who painted the sign and draped it on the ship, but no one comes to our door.

The next morning on the television news, we're surprised to see other people have done the same as us. Most of the other ships have huge signs made of drop sheets, tarps, or bedsheets draped on them. And every sign gets removed again. But the photos exist and are spread all around on social media, are shown on television, and appear in newspapers. People have now started to gather in front of the ships, carrying their own placards with similar wording. The movement is gaining momentum.

"Maybe our government would be prepared to bring them here," I say hopefully.

Mum is skeptical.

"I don't think you can save them, Jilda. I doubt Tasmania will welcome lots of animals as well as dealing with all these new people," says Mum.

"A lot of Tasmanians really care about the environment," says Rosa. "Look at all the people getting involved with placards and signs."

"What about quarantine?" says Mum. Sometimes I wish she wasn't so practical. She thinks of everything.

"Well, they would do their stint in quarantine, and then be let out," I say.

"Maybe Tasmania can't take *all* the animals from Levy Archipelago, but I'm sure we can find out who would," Jade says.

"Maybe some other countries will accept some of the animals," I suggest. "Taking several hundred or even more each, say?"

Mum looks at all of us.

"I doubt any government would care about another country's animals that much," says Mum. "And Levy Archipelago's government doesn't exist anymore, so you can't appeal to them to help you."

"I'm sure their governor will still care," says Jade. "And he'd have connections in lots of different countries, from when he used to be in charge. Maybe we could approach him."

"How much longer do you think the animals can live there?" Mum asks.

"A couple of years at the most I'd say, from what Marta and Simone said, but then that'd be it. The islands will be covered completely," I say.

"Oh dear," says Mum. "That's unthinkable." Mum is an animal lover after all.

"So the priority is to get them off, no matter what," I state firmly.

Jade looks at me admiringly.

"I agree," says Mum, "but it won't be you doing it."

Rosa and I catch each other's eyes. We know exactly what the other is thinking.

Our mum is an activist from way back. As is Dad. Our eyes say we'll do whatever it takes to get them to support us.

Chapter Sixteen
Gap Year Shore

Ever since then we've been campaigning to save the animals. Jade's parents finally agree for her to stay on longer—it is her gap year after all, and she's doing something very worthwhile with it. There are loads of long phone calls before it happens, including an extended Skype session with Mum convincing them she is doing her best to look after their daughter, taking the laptop around the house to show them where Jade is staying. They can't believe our view from the lounge-room windows, especially with the two huge ships filling the space. People who've never been to Hobart just don't realize what a beautiful place it is. Jade sends their luggage and the Tassie souvenirs she bought at the Salamanca Markets by sea mail, and promises she'll return home once our campaign is successful. She's so positive— she says "once," not "if."

Meanwhile, we all decide we should be doing more to help house the refugees, Marta and Jonas in particular. We find out they are camping in one of the local schools, and after all the documentation is completed, they move in with us. Despite their protestations they are putting us out, we know they really appreciate being in a real home once more.

I move out of my bedroom again and back into Rosa's. I decide I'd like to sleep on a mattress on the floor this time, rather than having poor Rosa put up with me tossing and turning all night, and anyway, I've almost become used to sleeping on the floor after the experience on the boat. I'll be able to sneak out sometimes to see Jade in the lounge room too, without disturbing Rosa, when everyone else in the house is sound asleep. We move my computer desk in and put it side by side with Rosa's, but we have to move Rosa's bookshelf out into the hall. It looks okay there. On top of the bookshelf we place the small wooden turtle and seahorse Mum had bought for us at the markets on that fateful day of the shore excursion when they were blissfully unaware of what was happening to me on the ship.

The schools finally reopen as the refugees begin to be housed, so Rosa and I have to juggle our campaign to save the animals with going to school. We're flat-out. Jade keeps at it all the time we're at school, or doing our homework, keeping the momentum going, and Marta and Jonas help out when they're not busy trying to find jobs. We hold rallies outside Parliament House on Saturday mornings where the Salamanca crowd can see and support us, and we write letters to the newspapers and whoever we think might help. We start a dedicated Facebook page to update followers of our progress. There is increasingly more interest, but nothing concrete is happening yet.

The Tasmanian government finally says we have to be realistic, and they can't accept thousands of pigs, chickens, cats, and dogs, but would be willing to take a share if we can find other countries that will take some as well and spread the load. Through Marta and Jonas, we approach their old governor, who is at first cautious but is won over by our enthusiasm for the idea.

By sending letters and emails and using the former governor of Levy Archipelago's contacts, we approach the governments of different countries around the Pacific region near Levy Archipelago, including Fiji, Samoa, Tonga, New Caledonia, Vanuatu, and others, and can't believe it when most of them agree to each take a thousand pigs and chickens, and will even pay us for them. None of them are interested in the cats and dogs, though. With countries willing to accept some of the animals, we now have to make it happen. And we need to think more about the cats and dogs.

Rosa, Jade, Marta, Jonas, and I approach Greenpeace and Animal Rights, and both organizations say they support us, but we have to realize that most of the pigs and chickens will still ultimately be killed for food if they are rescued anyway, so what's the use of going to all the effort of saving them from the rising waters. I reply that would have been their original fate on Levy Archipelago too, but now that the islands have been evacuated, at least this way their deaths will not be by panicked drowning and for no reason. If they are rescued, they can live a relatively pleasant life a little longer until their final destiny.

Representatives of both organizations say they can see my point and promise they will match us dollar for dollar in our bid to raise funds for saving the animals. With the promised sale price for the animals by the participating island countries, the numbers are starting to look possible.

We start a crowdfunding campaign to raise money to send a ship to collect the animals. Jade gets her parents and contacts in America involved too and encourages people over there to contribute. Her parents are supersupportive from the start, which helps Mum and Dad become a bit less skeptical. We don't know how much money to set as a goal, and we know if we don't reach that target we won't get a cent of the pledges, as that's how crowdfunding works. So we decide to try and raise fifty thousand dollars as a start.

We call our campaign "Pig Patrol," and have a hashtag to match, and can't believe how quickly the money pledges start arriving. Within a month we have our fifty thousand, and the figures just keep rising. By the time the campaign closes, we've raised one hundred thousand dollars. That means we now have three hundred thousand dollars for our cause, due to Greenpeace and Animal Rights both matching us dollar for dollar, plus we will have the money the different governments will give us to pay for the pigs and chickens when they receive them. The Tasmanian government consents to the release of one of the decommissioned cruise ships for the journey, and after hours of heated discussion, forcing them to imagine how they would feel if their pets werc lcft to drown, they agree to take all the dogs and cats as no one else will. However, they stipulate that while the pets are in quarantine they must be neutered and vaccinated, with the costs offset by the income from our farmers buying up the pigs and chickens. Only the healthy pets will be returned to their owners, so we must be realistic.

Rosa, Jade, and I beg to be allowed to go on the rescue mission. Jonas is to be the expedition leader, as he knows the waters so well, but Marta doesn't want to come, as she doesn't think she could bear to see her homeland again in such circumstances.

After much pleading, the government gives us the go-ahead to join the expedition—on the proviso our parents give their permission—as they concede the whole rescue is only occurring because of us and so we deserve to be a part of it. When we tell Mum and Dad the government is behind us, at first they forbid us to go. They say they're so proud we've gotten the project as far as it is, but they aren't going to let us take off to sea without them, especially as their emotions are still so raw from when I was missing for all that time. Finally, after days and nights of begging, tears, and promises of eternal good behavior, and everything else we can possibly think of, our parents—after discussing it with Jade's parents—agree we have earned the right because of our hard work and commitment. They trust Jonas after getting to know him so well through living with us, and know we'll be safe with him due to his familiarity with the ocean.

Chapter Seventeen
Ship and Shore

Mum and Dad, Marta, and thousands of supporters, mostly from Levy Archipelago, but also lots of Hobart locals, come to the docks to see us off. Some of them wave Levy Archipelago flags, and others wave long ribbons of brightly colored crepe paper in the colors of their flag. When we sail away from the pier, we can't believe the size of the crowd that is there to wish us well on our journey. Jade, Rosa, and I wave and wave until it feels like our arms are about to fall off, and then when the figures on the wharf are so tiny we can no longer distinguish them, we turn and face out to sea.

It's strange traveling on a decommissioned cruise ship, and the quarters we stay in are basic to say the least—nothing at all like when we set off on our cruise ship adventure from Sydney almost a year ago. But we're so proud of what we're about to do.

After a few days at sea, we arrive in the vicinity of Levy Archipelago. We've had a rough trip, and I'm glad I've got heaps of Mum's seasickness tablets, which I keep taking to keep the nausea at bay. Luckily they're helping quite a bit. I learned I'm prone to queasiness the hard way not all that long ago on that other fateful voyage, but I'm certainly not going to let my seasickness hold me back from doing what I've come to do on this important trip. Rosa and Jade, on the other hand, seem to be some of those lucky people who don't suffer from seasickness too much. Rosa keeps teasing me about how green I look, but Jade holds my hand and sympathizes.

Peering through Mum's binoculars she lent us for the trip, I can just make out several low-lying bumps in the distance.

"Is that them, Jonas?" asks the captain.

"Yes," says Jonas, quietly. His eyes are misting over, and his voice cracks.

We're counting on Jonas—being a fisherman, he'll know what the islands look like from way out in the ocean. We really can't afford to make a mistake and go off course in this vast region.

Finally we get up close. The water level has obviously risen. Many of the lower houses are now below the waterline, only their roofs showing above the waves, and water is lapping at the steps of the houses higher up. No wonder Marta didn't want to come to witness this. It would be heartbreaking if it was your home.

The pier is now underwater too, so we can't moor the boat. But we've been half expecting that. Anchoring as close to shore as we possibly can, we're able to see thousands of dogs, cats, pigs and chickens have made it to the highest point around. Some cats and chickens have even climbed into trees, and snakes have twined themselves around branches. Huge expanses of webs that look like nets are straddling the treetops, keeping the spiders that have woven them safely above the waterline. It's clear waves have been rolling over the area. It is a vision of hell. The animals couldn't have lasted much longer, and I'm so glad we've made the effort to come.

I take heaps of photos to post on Facebook and Twitter so all our supporters will be able see what their generous donations have achieved. Some of the photos will be turned into postcards and prints, which are some of the goodies donators will get in return for their pledge. We're also going to make certificates with photos of individual animals for those who committed to a higher amount. Mum's workplace offered to print and laminate them as their contribution to the cause.

Now that we're so close, we realize how difficult it will be to rescue them—but that's what we've come here for.

"Remind us of the best way to tackle this, Jonas," says the captain.

Jonas has been giving us advice about what to do on the trip over, as the more efficiently we can help the better. We need to do it as quickly as possible and get going. We still have many islands to visit to complete our mission, and then return home with the Tasmanian share of the animal cargo.

"First of all we must keep as quiet as possible so as not to frighten them," replies Jonas. "We need them to stay calm. If they panic, we won't be able to catch them."

"What about eye contact?" I ask. "Should we look at them directly, or will that spook them?"

"Eye contact with the pigs is good. They're very intelligent animals and like to connect with people to build trust. Keep eye contact to a minimum with the others, though."

"Okay, cool. Here's some of the treats we brought them," I say, dragging one of the large sacks full of baby carrots we've carried with us to entice the pigs over to our ship, hoping the other animals will follow them. I use both hands to hold the neck of the sack, and am bracing my feet on the deck, trying not to strain my back. My stomach is rolling, but I'm determined not to let it stop me doing what I need to do. Jade comes over and helps me throw some of the carrots into the ocean between us and the shore. They float enticingly, bright orange against the blue water.

"We'll have to work in pairs to catch the pigs and dogs," says Jonas. "One will throw out a lasso, and then we'll need both rescuers to haul them in."

"What happens if we miss with the rope?" I ask.

"Maybe you can be my sidekick, Jilda, while I toss the lasso," says Jonas, but his voice is kind.

I'm not too disappointed, as I can see his point. I don't want to hold up the proceedings with too many attempts at hurling a rope. I wasn't *that* good at quoits when I was young.

"What about the chickens and cats?" I ask. I'm thinking I might be better at catching them.

"They'll very soon get waterlogged once they start swimming, so we have to get them in quickly. We must keep them really calm and rescue them fast once they're in the water," says Jonas. "The pigs and dogs will be able to swim for a longer period of time, so if different types of animals are close, grab the chicken or cat first, then get the dog or pig."

We really couldn't have done all this without Jonas and his local knowledge.

Small boats called tenders are let down from the ship, and one by one we start to rescue the animals. It will take us a couple of days to get them all, as there are literally thousands of them and only twenty of us. I work alongside Jonas, and Jade and Rosa team up with other rescuers. I'm so impressed at the empathy Jonas has with the animals. They swim toward him, as if they know he's trying to help them, their eyes glowing and hopeful. Some of them are fearful and skittish, though, but trusting. I can see the panic in the chickens, as their eyes are darting furiously and they're flapping their wings madly.

Together, Jonas and I drag the animals into the tender. The pigs are incredibly heavy, but most are willing to help us pull them in, so their trotters scrabble on the sides of the boat to get purchase, and then we heave them up over the sides. I grab them round their necks, and Jonas leans farther out and hoists them up by their haunches. We use a similar tactic for the dogs, who are really eager to get in. My muscles are aching after only the first hour, but adrenaline keeps me going. Jonas works tirelessly at a feverish pace, and I'm not going to let him down. I know I'll be sore tomorrow.

The chickens and cats are much easier to bring onto the boat, as they're so much lighter, but their feathers or fur are wet and their claws scratch us in their fright. The captain hunts around in his cabin and finds several pairs of long gloves, which help a lot. The chicken's squawking is loud, and between them, the meowing cats, the oinking pigs, and barking dogs, it's starting to sound like a wild menagerie on board. I feel guilty about the spiders and snakes, but I know we have to draw the line somewhere, as a ship full of scuttling spiders and slithering snakes would not be a pleasant place at all. Apart from that, none of us are snake handlers, and we certainly don't want to get bitten by a snake or spider during our rescue mission.

As soon as our tender is full of animals, we head back to the main ship and are winched up to off-load our cargo. When that's completed, the tender is set down in the water again and we repeat the process. I soon lose count of how many trips we make in the tender. We have to keep working through the night, as the animals keep swimming toward us in a constant stream. They sense we're here to help them and are making the most of the opportunity. Jade, Rosa, and I have to take a rest, though, as it's physically impossible for us to keep up the constant effort. But Jonas doesn't want to stop, so he pairs up with Rosa's partner, who also seems to have superhuman powers.

I lie down on my bunk for a few hours to get some rest, but my sleep is so disturbed by dreams of wet animals clambering all over me, I might as well be up and actually doing it. So I drag myself out of bed and shake Jade and Rosa awake. We return to the deck as dawn spreads its amazing red and orange streaks across the sky and sea. We're not morning people, so we don't often get to see the sunrise—but the scene is spellbinding. We hold hands, the three of us in a row. However, the sea full of swimming animals is such a surreal sight that it quickly consumes all our attention and energy.

Finally we've finished our rescue mission, after having moved from island to island in the archipelago rescuing animals from every single one. Levy Archipelago is now empty of livestock and pets, and our ship is full with barely room to move. Jonas had said there were a lot of animals on their islands, but to see so many of them all crowded into one space has put it all into perspective. He told us that a lot of the families had animals, so it all makes sense, but still….

After the rescue, we set off again to take the pigs and chickens to the different island countries who have agreed to purchase them. In other circumstances, it could have been a pleasure cruise, such are the tropical islands we visit. To think it wasn't all that long ago Mum, Rosa, and I had enjoyed day trips to some of these places before our ship was taken over.

But there is no relaxing on this ship. The strong smell of so many animals in such a confined space makes our eyes water, and it's so noisy that it's sometimes hard to think. We feed the animals, tipping cracked grain from huge hessian sacks into long troughs for the pigs and chickens, and dried pet food for the cats and dogs into other containers. We have to make sure they have enough to drink, and regularly clean out all their muck. We're really careful to keep the food and water troughs separate from the waste buckets to avoid contamination. It's lucky Jade and I had so much practice with bodily waste with all the sick passengers on the cruise, as a lot of what we have to deal with now is pretty similar! Rosa says she feels a bit squeamish as it's so overwhelming, but she's determined to do her bit to help keep the ship relatively sanitary.

As we arrive at each port, authorities are there to count off the number and type of animals they've agreed to, money changes hands, and we're soon on our way to the next destination. Finally we've relieved ourselves of all but the animals the Tasmanian government has agreed to take, and we head homeward.

As we round the Iron Pot and sail up the River Derwent toward Hobart, I can't help but compare the emotions to when I traveled up the river after our ship had been commandeered by the Levy government, realizing I would soon be home. I'm proud of what we've achieved in saving all these animals from the horrible fate of terrified drowning, and can't really believe Jade, Rosa, and I have played such a huge part in it. It doesn't really seem all that long ago that Rosa, Mum, and I had flown to Sydney to join our cruise to celebrate our sixteenth birthdays, but I feel much, much older and wiser now than when we left.

Thousands of spectators, politicians, and a media contingent are waiting on the docks for us. Mum and Dad are right at the front of the crowd and beaming—they're so excited and proud. They're relieved we're safely back, but they say it's nothing compared to the relief they felt when I came back the first time. We stay at the docks for hours and hours while authorities deal with the thousands of animals, and then head home, exhausted and filthy.

Now that our mission is over, Jade says it's time for her to go home. She knows she can't live with Mum, Rosa, Marta,

Jonas, and me forever. Her gap year is almost up, and her parents are desperate to see her.

I love every minute being with her, and it's heartbreaking to think she has to leave. She and I are really getting to know each other so well after all we've been through together now, and I know she feels about me exactly the same way I feel about her. Breaking up with Zac was the best thing I could have done. Who knows where Jade's and my relationship will go, but with modern technology we're determined to keep in touch and find out.

On the day of Jade's departure, I find it hard to stay positive. On the way out to the airport, we sit in the back seat, holding hands. Rosa and Mum chat away to each other, intentionally not including us in their conversation so we can be in our own private world until the last minute. I'm trying to imprint on my mind the exact feeling of Jade's fingers in mine, wondering when I'll be able to feel them again. Jade's fingers that can play the piano and braid my hair and weave magic on my skin. And tie ropes with protest signs from ships and drag pigs, dogs, cats, and chickens from the ocean.

Jade releases my hand and feverishly scrabbles around in her bag. She finds a little red velvet box and passes it to me, insisting I open it. Inside is a pair of silver earrings in the shape of dolphins. I suddenly notice Jade is not wearing any earrings today. Without a word, I pick up one of the dolphin earrings and put it in her earlobe, then take out one of my turtle earrings and slot it in her other ear. She retrieves the remaining earring from the box and slips it into my empty earlobe. We gaze deeply into each other's eyes, fully understanding the meaning of our actions.

When we finally have to say goodbye at the airport, we hug so tightly, breathing in each other's scent, not speaking. Our bodies tell us everything we need to know. I can't bear the finality of that word—"goodbye." Our lips part for one last, lingering, soft kiss.

Jade turns and waves as she crosses the tarmac, then stops at the top of the stairs just before she enters the plane. She pivots around completely to face the terminal—she won't be able to see me, but I can see her as she waves and waves and blows a big theatrical kiss. I blow one back. I don't want Jade to disappear from view, but suddenly she's gone. Mum puts her arm around me, and Rosa does too, from my other side. I feel so loved and protected, but at the same time I have never felt so utterly alone.

CHAPTER EIGHTEEN
WHAT NEXT?

THE SHIP that brought us to Hobart the first time has long since gone—apparently it went straight back into service as a cruise ship, as soon as all the original passengers' belongings were returned to them. News reports say nothing was missing, which is amazing considering the number of people on the ship. So it seems the only theft was of the ring on Levy Archipelago itself, before coming on board. We hear the cruise company tried to fine the Levy Archipelago government for loss and damage to their reputation, but we aren't sure what's happening there. It will probably be a long, drawn-out affair. The other nine ships have been sent back to the ship wrecking yard to be scrapped as per the initial plans for them.

We found out later that a tsunami in Levy Archipelago was the final straw that set the whole idea in motion. A huge wave had just trundled across the islands and kept going, because the islands were so low-lying. But a cruise ship had been in that day, which gave one of the archipelago leaders the idea to sail the entire population away together, as the ship just rose up on the massive tsunami wave and came back down again, undamaged.

He started organizing retired cruise ships to be fitted out to take as many passengers as physically possible. He was just one cruise ship short when someone bribed the supervisor in charge of the refurbishments to spill the beans about what was happening with the ships. He didn't have enough time for a final ship to be prepared in the ships' graveyard, so he had to immediately think of a desperate alternate plan. The plan for the hijacking of an existing suitable cruise ship to make up the numbers was conceived and implemented: my ship. The converted ships and the one I was on then converged on Levy Archipelago and took the entire population on board in one go and sailed to Australia.

Once the mass of humanity was temporarily housed and sheltered, the Tasmanian premier said population growth was just what Tasmania needed, and the people from Levy Archipelago would not be turned away. Being a regional center, Tasmania was in a good position to grant special visas for these genuine climate refugees who had come in desperation and in peace.

There are still regular protests by those who want the people of Levy Archipelago to leave. But the premier says an increased population does not take away jobs, that in fact it creates jobs, as more services are needed, more schools, shops, and houses need to be built, there is more spending power, and so on. And the new inhabitants bring all their different skills, ideas, and richness of culture. Of course, building for all these people will take time, and so meanwhile everyone who can and is willing is doing their bit to provide accommodation and jobs in different parts of Tasmania.

The people from Levy Archipelago are slowly but surely being provided with housing in rural areas to build up those areas economically and not put too much pressure on the main population centers. After their pets have been through their quarantine period, and have been neutered, vaccinated, and pronounced healthy, they are returned to their owners.

Marta and Jonas have settled into life in the coastal town of Primrose Sands, not that far from Hobart, where Jonas is once more working as a fisherman. Marta is pregnant again and glowing.

Jade and I are in contact every day, and usually several times a day, and our relationship, if anything, is getting closer despite the distance. Before our experiences on the ship and saving the animals, we had both been uncertain of our futures—but now she is sure she wants to be a nurse or even a doctor, and I really want to be an environmentalist.

And I would just love to visit a town with a name like "Kissimmee." Wouldn't you? I'm working hard at my part-time job at Mures and saving up—I've almost got enough for the airfare already.

This is probably a good spot to stop.

This is my story.

And it's all true.

Or it will be.

POST SCRIPT

ALTHOUGH THIS is a fictional story, and Levy Archipelago is a figment of my imagination, many islands around the world are at risk of inundation due to rising sea levels caused by global warming. One such nation is Kiribati, which has a "Migration with Dignity" policy. They are a communal nation, where everyone shares close bonds by blood or clan and have a strong connection to the land. Their government is trying to negotiate with other countries so that their population will have somewhere to go in the near future, as their nation is under threat from the ocean. They will be true environmental refugees, the victims of human activity not of their making. The world needs to wake up and take notice of the consequences of our actions, of the human ignorance and greed that have led us inexorably toward this dire situation.

The islands are very narrow and low-lying, and it is estimated that by 2030 they will start to disappear under the waves. Coral, stone, and concrete seawalls have failed to hold back the rising tides as they collapse under the strain. Houses have already had to be moved, and plants the locals depend on for food, such as taro and plantain, are dying due to salination of the groundwater. People rely on rainwater to drink as underground water sources become salty and undrinkable.

Primrose Sands, among other coastal areas in Tasmania, is becoming a victim of global warming too. The tides are reaching higher, and locals are beginning to be concerned.

Have a look at the website www.coastalriskaustralia to see how rising sea levels will affect different parts of Australia in the future. It is a sobering website to visit, but do.

VERITY CROKER loves being on the high seas, although she, like Jilda, suffers from seasickness. She grew up in Canberra, and has lived in several different regions in Australia, as well as in Scotland and China.

Verity enjoys writing, reading, walking, swimming, and planning her next travel adventure. She is a published author of books, poems, short stories, travel tales, and newspaper articles.

You can find Verity on:

Facebook: www.facebook.com/veritycrokerwriter
Twitter: @veritycroker
Website: www.veritycroker.wordpress.com

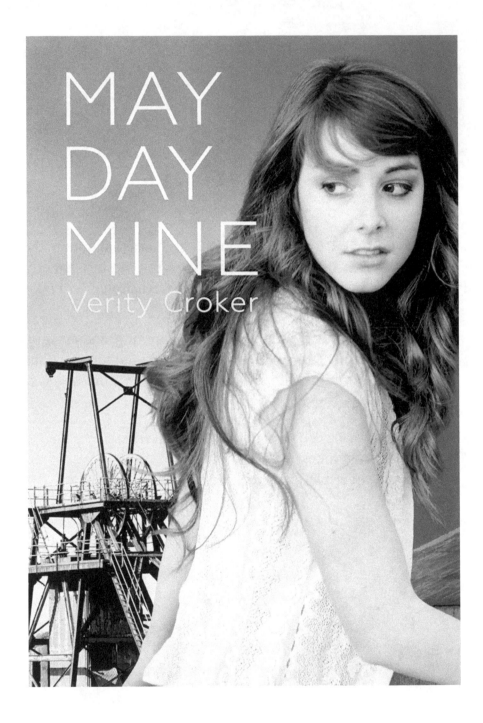

MAY
DAY
MINE

Verity Croker

Life in a small mining town can be like living in a fishbowl, where everyone knows everybody else's business. Fifteen-year-old Jodi's mother wants her father to quit his binge drinking and his dangerous job at the mine—even more so after a collapse leaves two miners dead and three trapped deep underground.

As tensions escalate both at home and around the town, Jodi seeks comfort with her friends but soon faces a double betrayal. Meanwhile, her ten-year-old brother Jake reacts by joining a gang of schoolyard bullies who engage in increasingly dangerous antics.

As Jodi struggles to gain autonomy over her life, she begins to discover the person she really is. But with everything around her spiraling out of control, it may not be the right time to let her family, friends, and ultimately the whole town know—no matter how much she wants to.

www.harmonyinkpress.com

Also from Harmony Ink Press

JO RAMSEY
MIDNIGHT
CHAT

Stay home tomorrow

www.harmonyinkpress.com

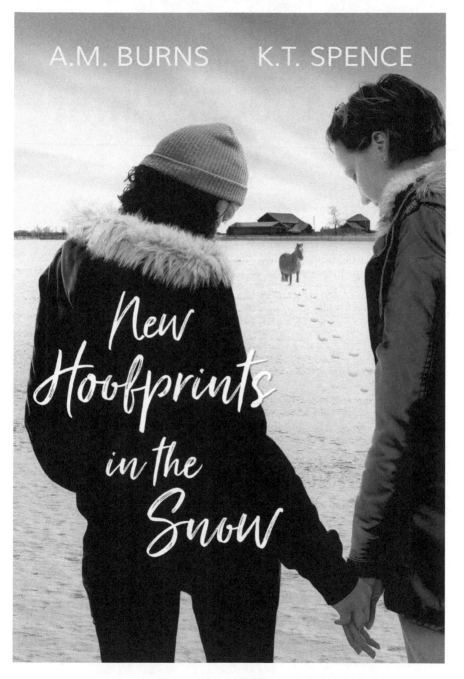

Also from Harmony Ink Press

SHIRLEY ANNE EDWARDS

Rage
to Live

www.harmonyinkpress.com

Also from Harmony Ink Press

www.Harmony Inkpress.com